W9-CEG-240

After the publication of *Ola* in 1932, the work of Ingri and Edgar Parin d'Aulaire has needed no introduction—their beautiful picture books have delighted countless children ever since.

Ingri Mortenson and Edgar Parin d'Aulaire met in Munich, where both were studying art. Ingri had grown up in Norway; Edgar, the son of a noted Italian painter, was born in Switzerland and had lived in Paris and Florence. Shortly after their marriage they moved to this country and began to create the beautiful children's books for which they became famous, including the 1939 Caldecott winner—*Abraham Lincoln.*

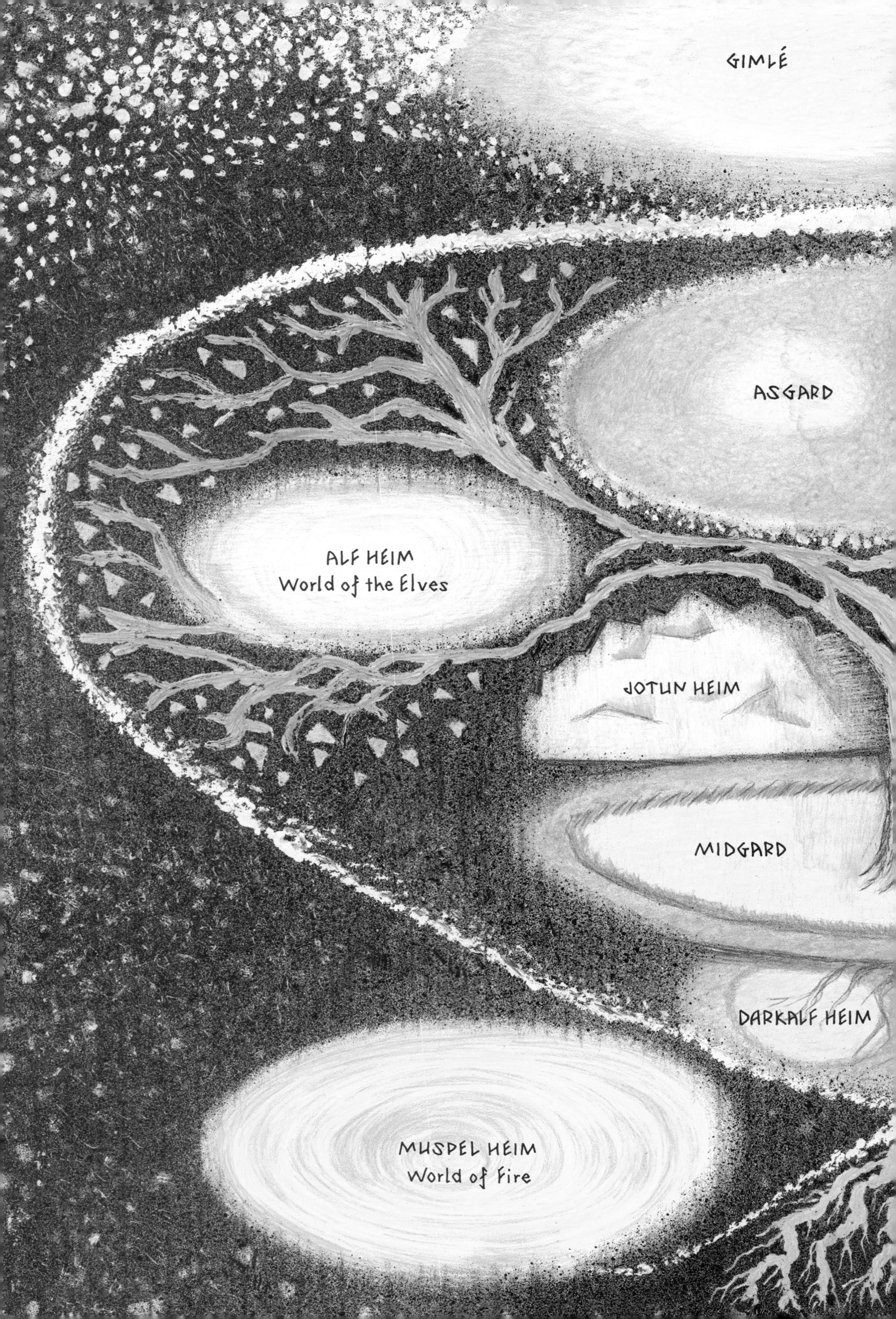

GIMLÉ

ASGARD

ALF HEIM
World of the Elves

JOTUN HEIM

MIDGARD

DARKALF HEIM

MUSPEL HEIM
World of Fire

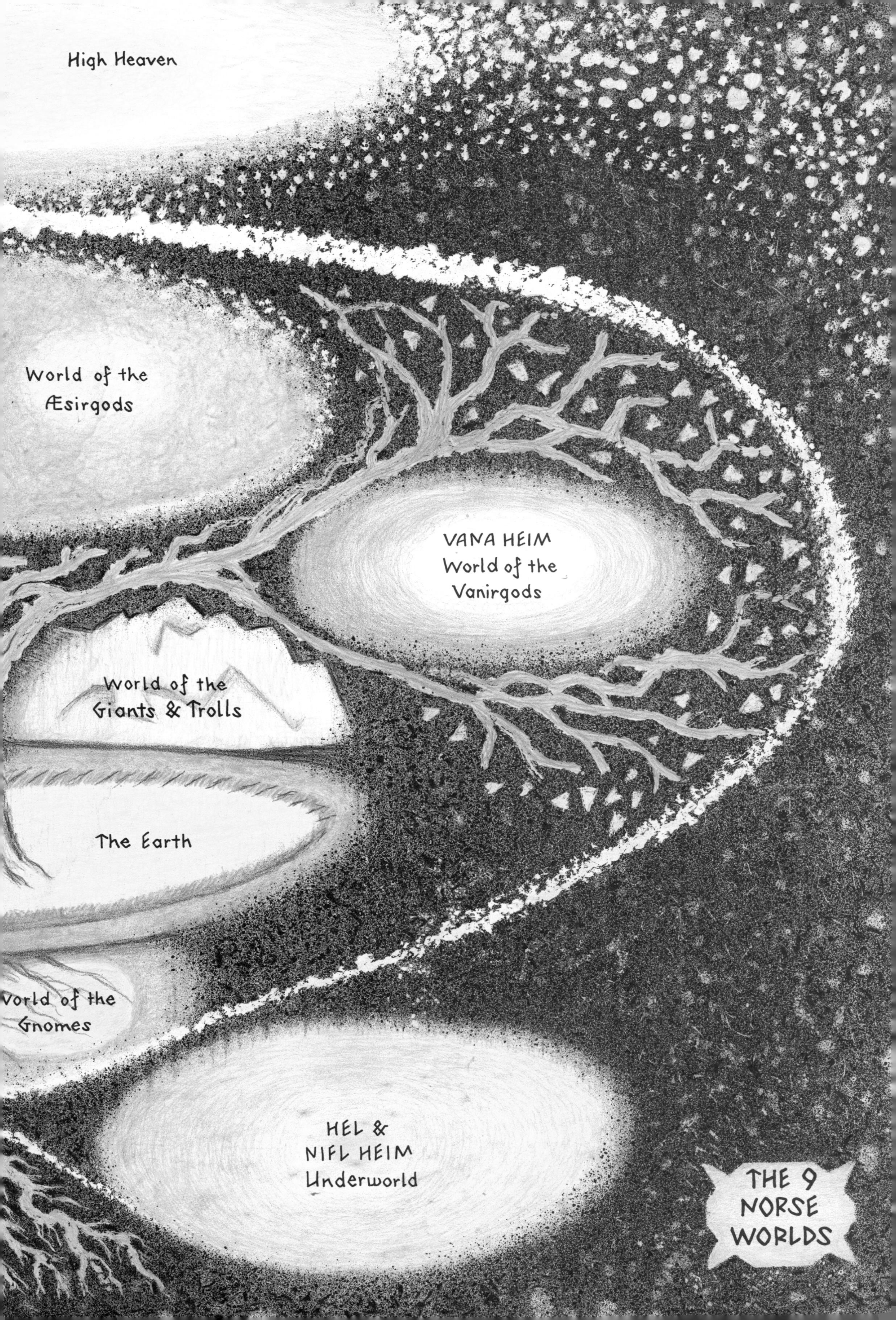

High Heaven

World of the
Æsirgods

VANA HEIM
World of the
Vanirgods

World of the
Giants & Trolls

The Earth

orld of the
Gnomes

HEL &
NIFL HEIM
Underworld

THE 9
NORSE
WORLDS

D'AULAIRES'

NORSE GODS and GIANTS

BRAGI
IDUNN
ULL
SKADE
GERD
FREY
NJORD
FREYA
HEIMDALL
SIF
THOR
NOSS
Modi
Magni

INGRI and EDGAR PARIN D'AULAIRE

D'AULAIRES' NORSE GODS and GIANTS

DOUBLEDAY

NEW YORK LONDON TORONTO SYDNEY AUCKLAND

Other books by Ingri and Edgar Parin d'Aulaire

ABRAHAM LINCOLN

BENJAMIN FRANKLIN

COLUMBUS

D'AULAIRES' BOOK OF GREEK MYTHS

D'AULAIRES' TROLLS

GEORGE WASHINGTON

POCAHONTAS

The authors are grateful for the assistance of Odd Nordland, Assistant Professor at the Institute for Nordic Languages and Literature at Oslo University, Oslo, Norway, and for the calligraphy by Martha Thompson.

Published by Doubleday, a division of
Bantam Doubleday Dell Publishing Group, Inc.
666 Fifth Avenue, New York, New York 10103

Doubleday and the portrayal of an anchor with a
dolphin are trademarks of Doubleday, a division of
Bantam Doubleday Dell Publishing Group, Inc.

Library of Congress Cataloging-in-Publication Data

d'Aulaire, Ingri, 1904–1980
d'Aulaires' Norse gods and giants.

Summary: A collection of Norse myths describing the exploits of the gods and goddesses of the Aesir beginning with the creation and ending when the gods and giants destroyed each other in battle.
1. Gods, Norse—Juvenile literature. 2. Mythology, Norse—Juvenile literature. 3. Giants—Mythology—Juvenile literature. [1. Mythology, Norse]
I. d'Aulaire, Edgar Parin, 1898–1986. II. Title.
III. Title: Norse gods and giants.
BL860.D355 1986 293'.13 86-11677

ISBN 0-385-23692-1 (pbk.)

3 4 5 6 7 8 9 10

TO THE MEMORY OF
MAY MASSEE
OUR OLD FRIEND

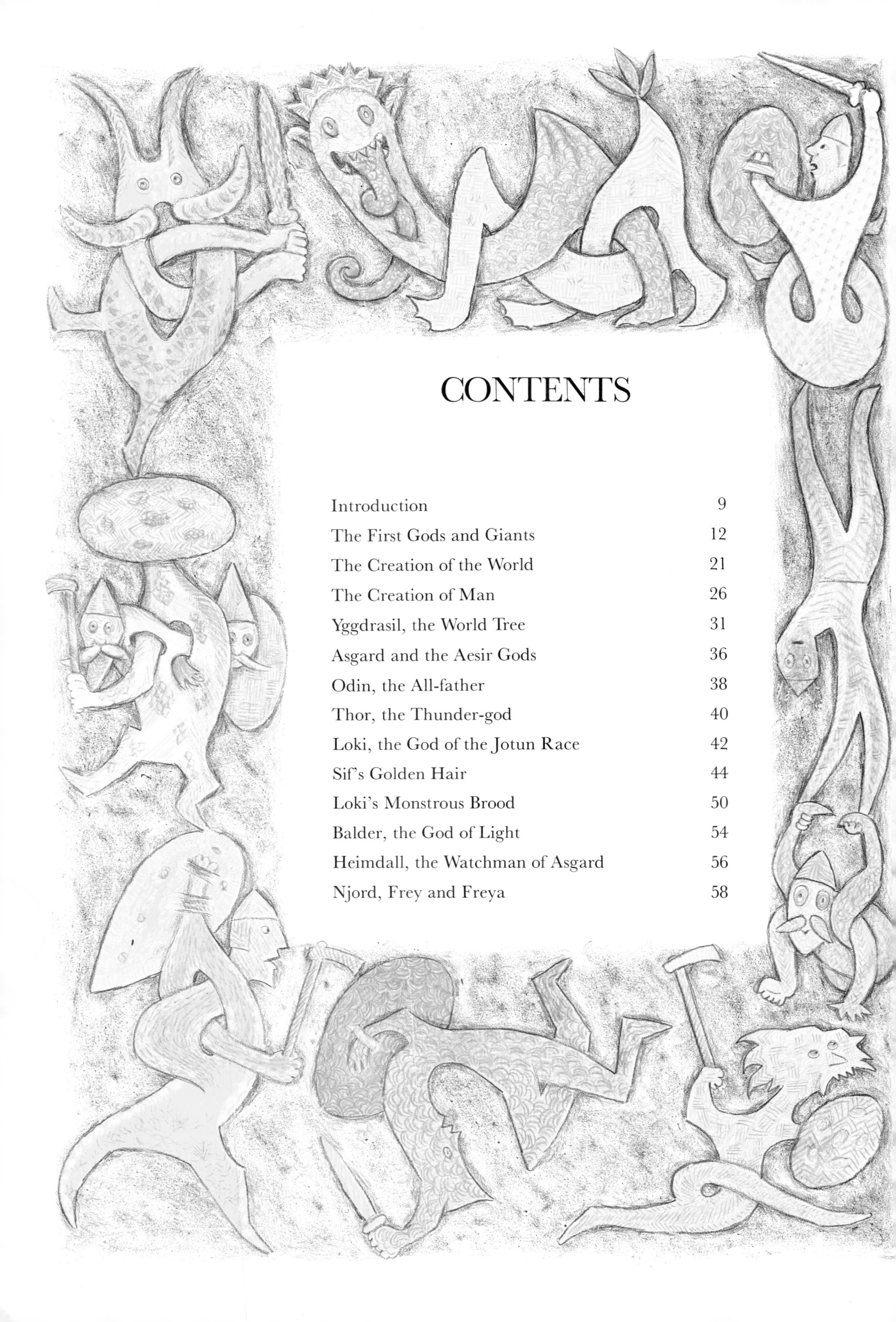

CONTENTS

Introduction	9
The First Gods and Giants	12
The Creation of the World	21
The Creation of Man	26
Yggdrasil, the World Tree	31
Asgard and the Aesir Gods	36
Odin, the All-father	38
Thor, the Thunder-god	40
Loki, the God of the Jotun Race	42
Sif's Golden Hair	44
Loki's Monstrous Brood	50
Balder, the God of Light	54
Heimdall, the Watchman of Asgard	56
Njord, Frey and Freya	58

Bragi, God of Poetry	64
Odin's Eight-legged Steed	68
The Valkyries and Valhalla	72
Frigg and the Goddesses	80
Freya's Wonderful Necklace	84
Idunn's Apples of Youth	87
Skade, the Ski-goddess	91
Frey and Gerd, the Jotun Maiden	96
The Theft of Thor's Hammer	100
Thor and the Jotun Geirrod	104
Thor and the Jotun Utgardsloki	108
Thor and the Jotun Rungnir	117
Thor and the Jotun Aegir	120
The Death of Balder	128
Loki's Punishment	137
Ragnarokk, the Destiny of the Gods	140
A New World	151
Reader's Companion	156

Introduction

WHEN the last ice age came to an end, the great glaciers that capped Northern Europe melted, uncovering a barren and rugged land. On the heels of the withdrawing ice came reindeer, wolves, bears, and foxes. They were pursued by hunters.

These men were forever struggling against Frost Giants, the cold-hearted spirits of the mountains and glaciers. But they found shelter in the valleys, where meadows grew lush and forests grew dense and deep. For thousands of years the beasts and the men who hunted them roamed throughout the north.

Then, from the east, burst a tribe of fierce horsemen. They stormed westward, settling new lands as they went. Led by a hulking, one-eyed chieftain, they spurred their horses on until at long last they were stopped by the crashing waves of the North Sea. They could go no farther, so they settled and made the land theirs.

Life in the north was hard for these new settlers. The Frost Giants sent bitter storms howling down from the mountains. Wild beasts, trolls and evil spirits lurked in the pathless forests, and cruel mermaids wrecked their ships. But the settlers were tough, and they were protected by their own gods, the Aesir, who had come with them from their faraway lands.

First among the Aesir gods was Odin, ruler of gods and men. His realm was made up of nine worlds: the worlds of the dead; of fire; of gnomes; of men; of giants; of elves; of the Vanir gods; of the Aesir gods; and the world with the roof of glittering stars, where all good souls would one day meet.

Through all these nine worlds grew the ash tree, Yggdrasil. Only as long as this tree flourished was the reign of the Aesir fated to last. Like plants, beasts, and men, the Aesir gods, too, one day must die.

A thousand years ago, when Christianity conquered the north, the Aesir gods perished. They met their destiny on the day of Ragnarokk, when they and the monsters of the mountains and glaciers destroyed each other. Soon they were almost forgotten in most of the lands where they had once been worshiped. All that remained of them were fragments in folklore and a few of their names that had been given to the days of the week.

Tuesday is named for Tyr, ancient god of the sword; Wednesday is Odin's day; Thursday is Thor's; and Friday is the day of Freya, goddess of love.

Though the Dutch, Germans, Franks, and Saxons forgot these old gods and their battles with ice-age monsters, the Norse did not. Through the long winter nights Norsemen, young and old, would gather around their smoky fires in their long halls to hear the stories and songs of their bards.

To keep the trolls and giants away, they used to paint Thor's hammer on their barn doors and the dragons' heads carved on their church portals were there to frighten away the heathen spirits. To this very day, in lonely valleys, the people may tell of meetings with trolls and gnomes and other strange creatures of the past.

On the outlying island of Iceland, where volcanoes and glaciers stand side by side, the memory of the ancient Aesir gods was kept alive longer than anywhere else. Passed on, word by word, from father to son, these stories were at last written down in two books: the Poetic Edda and the Prose Edda.

The Poetic Edda is a collection of old Norse verse, set down in the tenth and eleventh centuries. The Prose Edda, a collection of myths and fanciful tales, was written by Snorri Sturluson about the year 1200.

From these two great Icelandic books, and from scattered folklore and songs, we know today how the ancient Norsemen thought the world of their ancestors was created, how it flourished, and how it came to an end.

The First Gods and Giants

EARLY in the morning of time there was no sand, no grass, no lapping wave. There was no earth, no sun, no moon, no stars. There was Niflheim, a waste of frozen fog, and Muspelheim, a place of raging flames. And in between the fog and fire there was a gaping pit—Ginungagap.

For untold ages crackling embers from Muspelheim and crystals of ice from Niflheim whirled around in the dark and dismal pit.

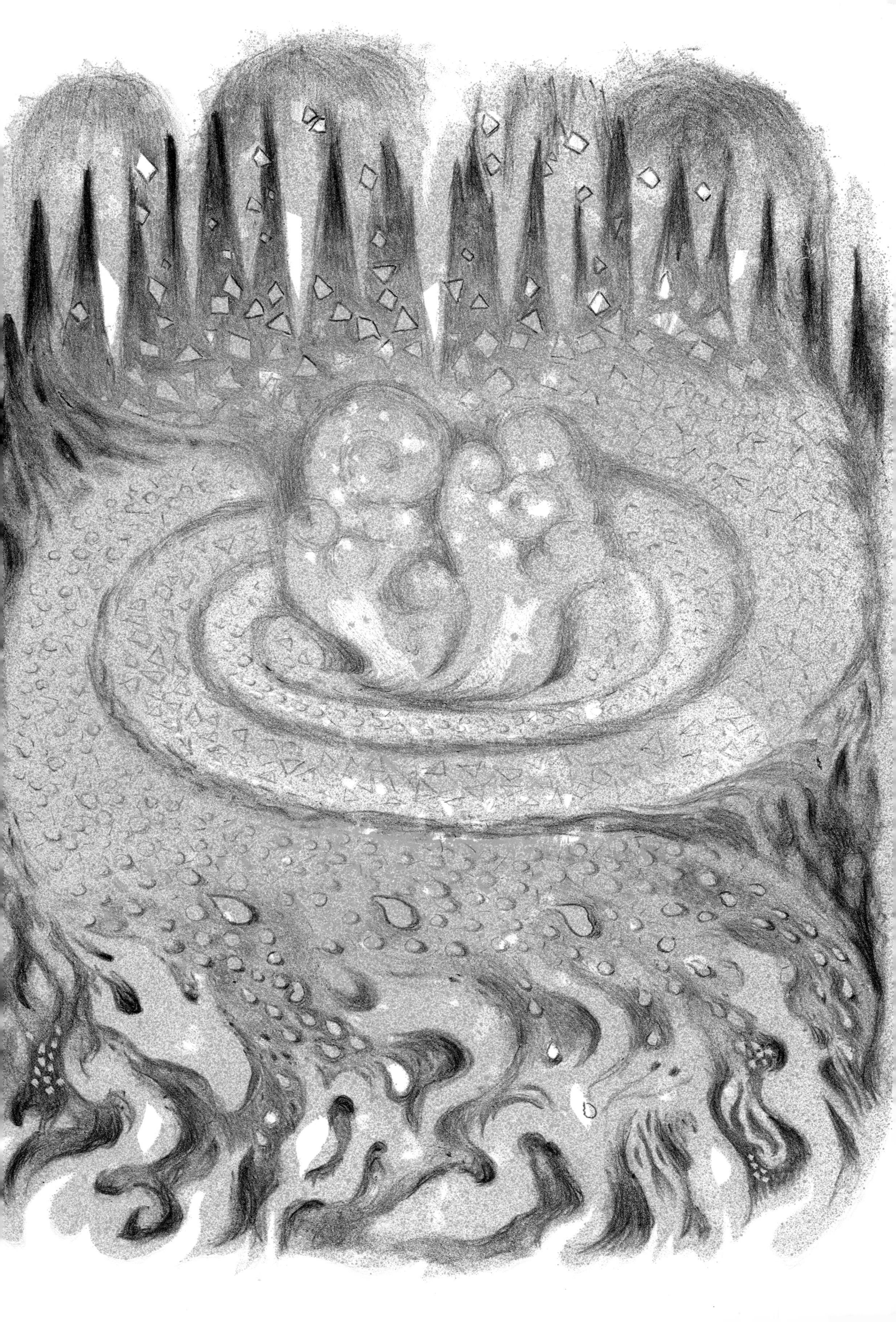

As they whirled together, faster and faster, fire kindled a spark of life within the ice. An enormous, ugly shape rose roaring from Ginungagap. It was the frost giant, Ymir, first of the race of the jotuns. At his side a hornless ice cow came mooing from the pit.

Together jotun and cow lived on the rim of Ginungagap. The jotun

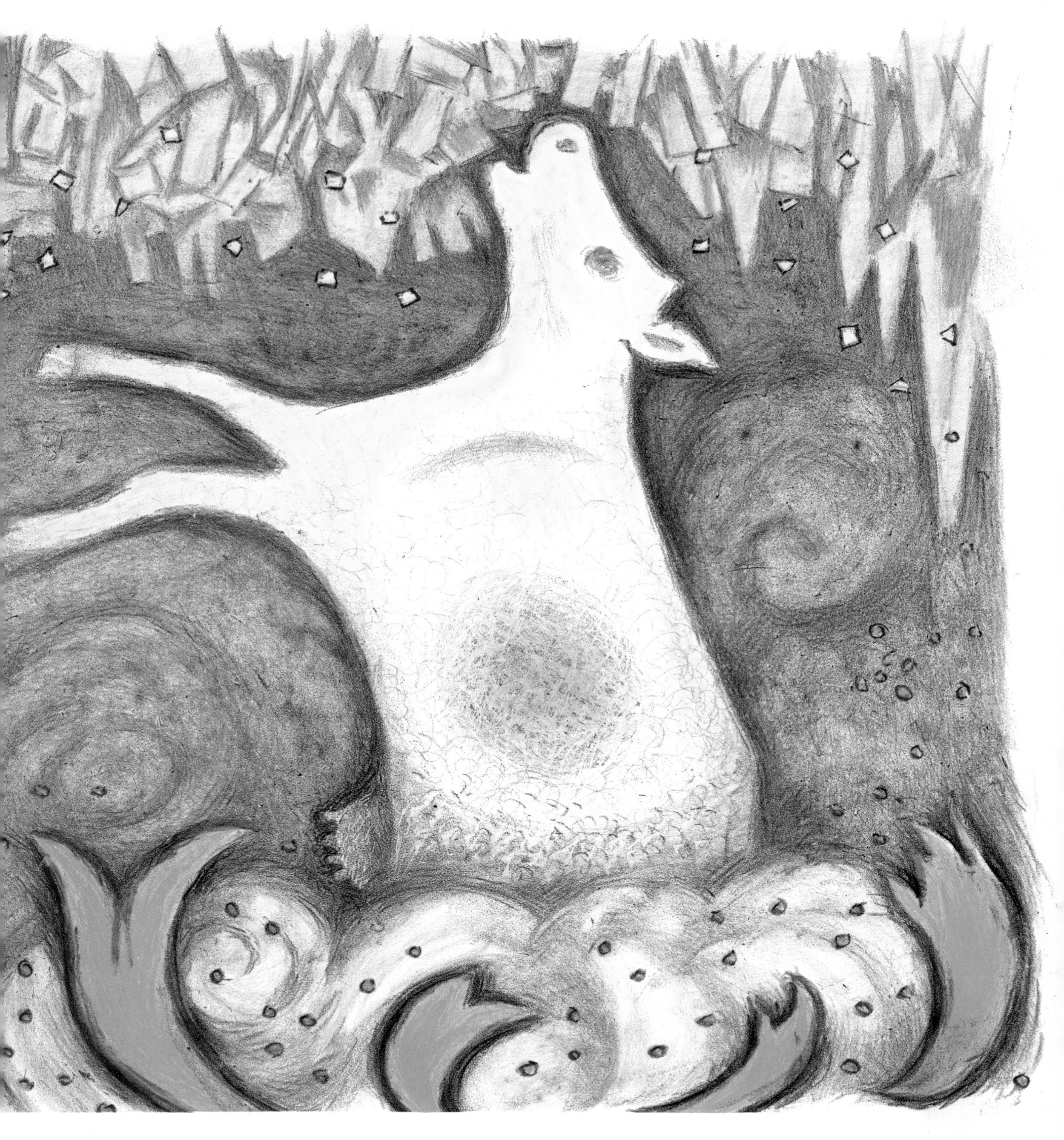

did not lack for food. Four rivers of snow-white froth flowed like milk from the huge ice cow's udder, and Ymir drank and drank and grew to a towering height.

As for the cow, she found plenty of food licking the salty brim of Ginungagap.

For a long time there were only Ymir and the cow. Then Ymir fell into a deep sleep. While he slept, a male and a female jotun came to life in the warmth in his left armpit, and a troll with six heads sprouted from his feet. These monstrous creatures grew quickly and had offspring of their own. They were all big and rough, and Ymir was the biggest and

wildest of them all.

The ice cow also brought about life. As she licked and licked, her tongue grew warm, for she had to lick hard to make enough food for Ymir and his brood. Then, under her warm tongue, a head of hair sprouted on the briny brim, and as she went on licking, a face appeared.

The cow went right on licking. Shoulders and chest came forth, then legs, and, at last, out stepped a whole new creature! He was straight and quite handsome—not ugly like the jotuns and trolls. He had a son who was even more handsome, and the son took for his wife a beautiful jotun maiden; for it sometimes happened that an ugly frost giant would have a lovely daughter.

She bore her husband three sons who were so fair that a radiance spread from them and lit up the darkness around them. They were the first of the great Aesir gods; their names were Odin, Hoenir, and Lodur—Spirit, Will, and Warmth. They were high and very holy, and they had the power to create a world.

But before the three gods could begin to create, they had to get rid of the frost giant, Ymir. He had always been wild, and old age had made him worse. So the three young Aesir gods went against the age-old jotun.

They slew Ymir and pushed his huge hulk into Ginungagap. So much brine flowed from his wounds that it filled the pit and flooded over the rim. The cow and all Ymir's offspring were drowned except for two—a very strong jotun and his mate. They clambered up onto ice floes and went to live on the wild outer shores of the sea made by Ymir's brine. The Aesir did not pursue them, and almost right away this icebound wilderness, Jotunheim, was teeming with their offspring.

These uncouth jotuns and trolls hated the Aesir for what they had done to their kinsmen. They watched as the handsome gods made a new world, and raged among themselves.

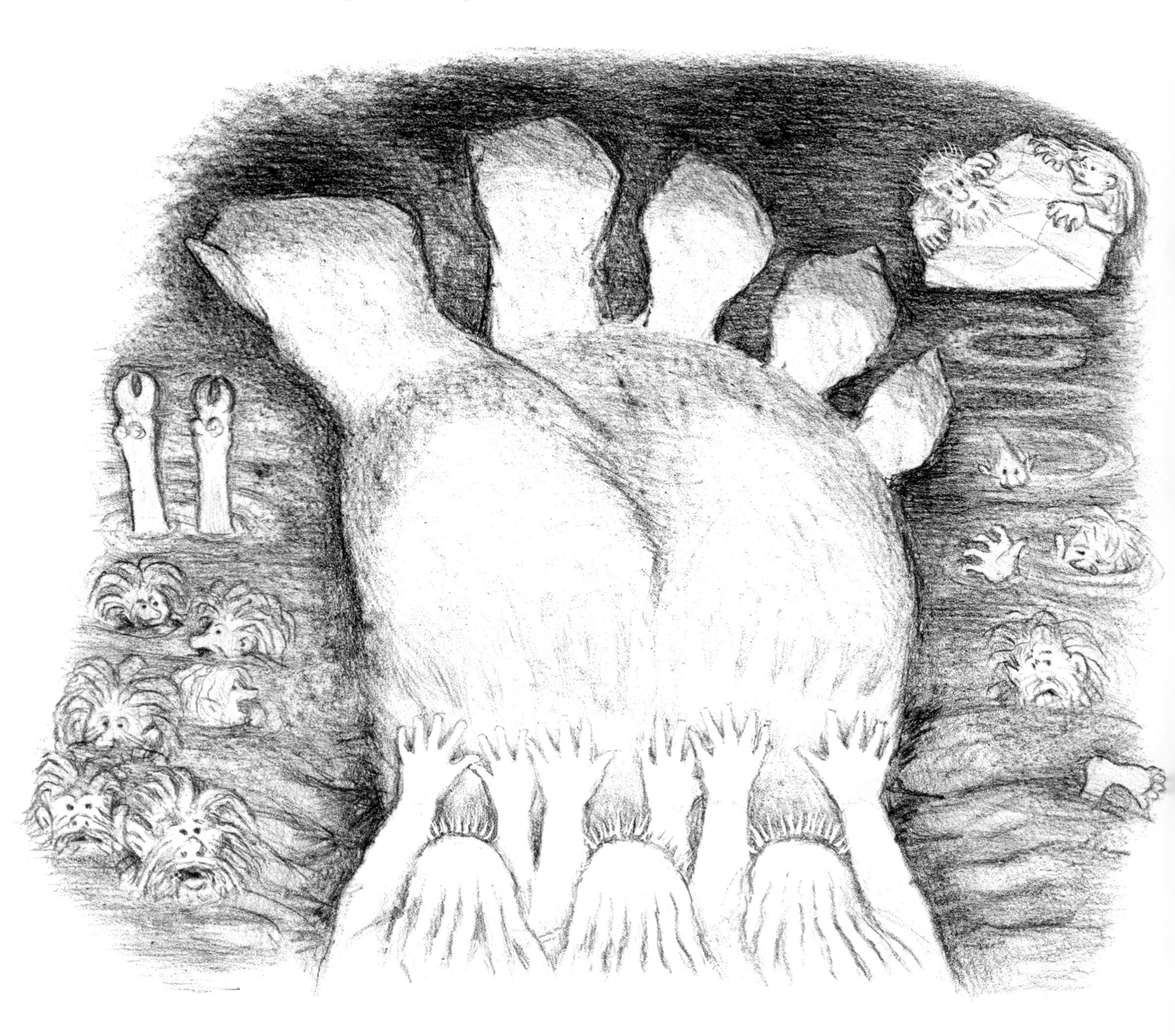

The Creation of the World

THE AESIR raised Ymir's body out of the sea and made Midgard, the earth, from it. Ymir's flesh became the soil, his bones the mountains, his teeth boulders and stones. They pushed desolate Niflheim deep underground where its icy fog could not freeze the earth. And over land and sea they set Ymir's huge skull as the dome of the sky so the sparks from Muspelheim would not set the new world afire.

They caught some of the sparks and fastened them to the dome and these became the sun, the moon, and the stars. Still, there was neither day nor night, for the sun and the moon did not move—they were fastened to their places. So Odin, Hoenir, and Lodur made two teams of horses, put the sun and the moon each into a cart behind them, and set the horses trotting across the sky. First came the moon. The manes of his horses were covered with hoarfrost, and the icy crystals spread a silvery light over Midgard, the earth. Then came the sun. She was so bright that she bathed the earth with a golden light, and she was so hot that the Aesir had to tie bellows to the flanks of her horses to keep them from being burned.

But the jotuns and trolls were creatures of darkness. They hated the light. Some of them could change their shapes at will, so two of them, disguised as wolves, sprang up on the dome of the sky. They ran after the sun and the moon, trying to catch and devour them, and the horses ran for their lives. They ran round and round the sky, always with the wolves at their heels, never daring to pause. And so there were noon and dusk and dark and dawn on earth.

Related to the Aesir were some other gods, the Vanir gods. They lived in a neighboring world, Vanaheim, and ruled over rain and soft winds. They sent gentle showers to earth.

As rain fell and the warm rays of the sun shone on Ymir's gray bones, the stubble of his beard sprouted as green grass and spread over valleys and glens. His hair grew into deep forests. Birch, ash, and oak unfolded their leaves, and forests of pine and fir grew dense and dark. It was a beautiful, fresh, green earth, and now the Aesir began to people it.

First they made the light elves, shining creatures, bright as sunbeams and light as leaves. They were gentle and good and flew about on gossamer wings. Their homes were not on earth, but high up in the air in the shimmering world of Alfheim, which the Aesir gods made for them.

There were worms burrowing deep underground in Ymir's ore-laden veins. The Aesir changed these into gnomes and gave them tools to mine the precious metals. Soon the caves rang with the sound of hammers and chisels. The gnomes were not friendly. They were grumpy and tricky little men who hobbled along and spoke with shrill, echoing voices. Their faces were pale as mushrooms, for they lived underground and the sun

never shone upon them. But they were marvelous miners and smiths, and they kept the Aesir well supplied with gold, silver, and iron.

Then the Aesir made sprites and spirits to inhabit the land and the sea and care for every hillock, every mountain, every lake and waterfall.

And, last, they made fish to gambol in the sea, birds to soar in the sky, and animals to run about and prowl in the fields and forests. The Aesir looked around, and they were pleased with their work. They had animals to hunt and fish to catch. The only thing they did not have was someone who would worship them. So they decided to create man.

But how was he to look?

The Creation of Man

ONE DAY, as the three young Aesir walked along the seashore, their eyes fell upon two little trees, an ash and an alder, standing side by side. In these two trees they saw the makings of mankind—straight as gods and tough as wood.

But the ash and the alder were only trees; they had no souls, they could neither think nor move, and the sap that flowed beneath their bark was cold. So together the three gods blew life into the trees. Odin gave them souls, Hoenir gave them the will to think and move, and Lodur gave them feeling and warm red blood. Slowly the ash and the alder turned and twisted into a man and a woman.

Still, a naked, nameless man is not far above an animal, and the

Aesir wanted human beings to be the greatest of all their creations. So they gave them names and loaned them their own cloaks until they could learn to make clothes for themselves. They named the man Ask (Ash) and the woman Embla (Alder) after the trees from which they had been created.

As a birth gift they gave them the whole earth for their home, and, to protect them against the onslaughts of the wild jotuns in Jotunheim, they made a fence of Ymir's eyebrows and placed it around the earth.

Then the three gods made a home for themselves high up above the tallest mountains and set up a shimmering rainbow as a bridge between earth and Asgard, their home.

From Asgard they watched over Ask and Embla and all their children.

The first descendants of Ask and Embla were not handsome. Their skin was rough like bark, their joints gnarled. They ate wild plants, hunted animals with clubs, and wrapped themselves in furs to keep out the cold. They lived in hovels, had no manners at all, and their eyes were downcast and dull.

Their grandchildren were better in every way. They tilled the soil, lived in houses, sailed the seas. They ate well-baked breads and dressed in shapely clothes, and their shoulders were broad, their cheeks rosy, and their eyes lively.

Their great-grandchildren were finer still. They were fair and handsome and sat at leisure in great halls, dressed in fine woolens and snow-white linens. They ate roasts from silver platters and sipped sweet mead from crystal goblets and ornate drinking horns.

They had manners, for Odin himself told them how to behave.

In the disguise of a wise old wanderer he often walked among men. A wide-brimmed hat shaded his face; a dark blue cloak, set with sparkling stars, hid his huge chest. He walked about the earth, testing the hospitality of people, for hospitality was very important to men who lived far apart in wild and roadless lands.

When he was welcomed to hall or hovel he seated himself by the fire and talked to the people.

"Your friend's friends shall be your friends; your friend's foes shall be your foes. Tread down the path to your friend's house and don't let it grow over with weeds," he said.

"Always keep your door open to the tired traveler. The man who comes to your house with shivering knees needs a place by the fire and dry clothes and warm food.

"When you enter the house of a stranger, look into cupboards and dark corners to see if a foe might be hiding. Then take the seat that is offered you, and listen more than you speak. For then no one will notice how little you know.

"Always have a bite to eat before going to a feast; a hungry man is not a bright speaker.

"It's an unwise man who sits awake worrying all night. When morning comes he will be too tired to think and matters will be still more tangled."

And last, he always said, "Men die, cattle die, you yourself must die one day. There is only one thing that will not die—the name, good or bad, that you have made for yourself."

Thus Odin, the Aesir god, sat by the hearths and spoke, and the people listened. When he disappeared, they knew they had been listening to the voice of the High One, and they held his words sacred.

The human beings were thankful to the gods for having created them and for sending sunshine and rain to their fields, and they sacrificed to them and worshiped them in sacred groves and sanctuaries. The Aesir, in turn, were fond of mankind and watched over them and protected them against the jotuns.

But it was the three Fays of Destiny, the Norns, who decided the fate of every human being. Their names were Urd, Verdande, and Skuld, and they knew what was, what had been, and what was to be. To every newborn child they willed a life of luck or a life of misery, a short life or a long one, for the Norns spun a thread of life for every human being. Mostly it was a gray, coarse thread. But for farmers and freemen they sometimes spun a finer thread in a brighter color. And once in a while, for a hero or a great prince, they would spin a thread of gleaming gold.

Nobody knew where the Norns had come from, or whether they were fairies or of the jotun race. But even the Aesir had to bow to the will of Urd, Verdande, and Skuld, for the Aesir were not immortal gods. They too must die when the Norns decreed it, like everybody and everything else.

Yggdrasil, the World Tree

THE THREE NORNS lived at the foot of an enormous ash tree which grew right from the middle of the earth. It was so tall that its top touched the vault of the sky; its branches stretched out over all the earth, and its huge roots went down to the deepest depth. The dew that dripped from its evergreen leaves made flowers spring up all over Midgard, the earth. As long as the ash tree stood, the world of the Aesir would last, for it was Yggdrasil, the world tree.

On the topmost branch of Yggdrasil an eagle sat and fanned the air with his wings, making the leaves rustle as if they were breathing. With his sharp eyes he scanned the four corners of the world, and a little bright-eyed hawk perched on his beak, helping him to keep watch.

While the eagle was guarding Yggdrasil, a dreadful dragon lay far underground in dismal Niflheim, gnawing away at its roots. It was Nidhogg, the dragon of destruction, trying to destroy the world tree. Ratatosk, a busybody squirrel, scampered up and down the tree, carrying abuse back and forth between the eagle and the dragon.

Many creatures made their homes in the tree and it suffered much damage. Worms bored holes in its bark, deer nibbled at its foliage, and all the birds in the world built their nests from its twigs. Still the world tree thrived, because the three Norns cared for it. At the foot of the tree there was a sacred pool with snow-white swans swimming on it. Every morning the three Norns scooped water from the pool and sprinkled it upon the tree. This water was so magic and so pure that it healed all of Yggdrasil's wounds.

As the population on earth had increased, so had the godly population. Odin, Hoenir, and Lodur had taken for their wives many beautiful jotun maidens who had made them the fathers of strong young gods and lovely goddesses. Odin himself was the father of nine of the great new gods. They were Thor, Balder, and Hod, Tyr, Heimdall and Bragi, Hermod, Vidar and Vali.

They were all high and holy, but Odin came to be first among the Aesir. To gain greater power, he hanged himself on Yggdrasil's windswept branches, Odin sacrificed to Odin. For nine nights and nine days he hung there suffering in silence, staring at the twig-strewn ground without closing an eye.

On the ninth night he saw that the twigs that dropped from Yggdrasil fell into shapes which spelled out words and symbols. Thus he discovered the magic of the runic letters, which he would share with the Aesir and wise men on earth. Whoever could master the runic alphabet and carve the magic letters on wood or stone possessed great powers. Through reading and writing men could now send their words to others who were far away. They could even share their thoughts with those who were not yet born.

But the runes were dangerous, too; there were evil symbols that witches and sorcerers sometimes used to put a spell on a man or on his cattle.

When Odin came down from Yggdrasil, he was the All-father, the father of Aesir and men, wisest of them all. His two brothers, Hoenir and Lodur, with whom he had created the world of the Aesir, faded into the background to make more room for him. And all the other Aesir turned to him for advice just as children turn to their father.

From then on Yggdrasil was Odin's sacred tree. The sacrifices made to him were hung from its branches, and it was at the foot of the great tree that he gathered the other Aesir around him every morning. There they sat in council and loudly debated what was just or unjust, and decided the course of Asgard and earth. Everyone had his say, and when a matter of great importance was debated, even the Asynjer, the god-

desses, were called in.

When the council was over they mounted their horses and rode up the shimmering rainbow bridge to Asgard, their home, above the clouds. Flimsy as the rainbow bridge looked, it was the strongest of all bridges. The Aesir had made it with great care to keep the frost giants away, for the red in it was glowing fire that burned the icy feet of jotuns and trolls.

Asgard and the Aesir Gods

AT THE TOP of the rainbow bridge rose Asgard, gleaming like the sun. There were gold and silver everywhere—even the fence around it was made of golden posts and silver staves. The Aesir loved these beautiful metals, and the gnomes kept them well supplied.

In the middle of Asgard lay the heavenly green field of Ida. There the Aesir and their wives strolled about or played chess with golden

chessman on golden boards, and around the green stood their wonderful halls. Tallest of all the splendid buildings was a silver tower which the Aesir had built for Odin. On its top stood his throne, the Lidskjalf. From there he could see the whole world. He could watch what men and women were doing, what was going on deep underground. He could even see what the jotuns were up to in far away Jotunheim. None of the Aesir was allowed to sit on his high throne, but sometimes he would let Frigg, dearest of his wives, share it with him. So Frigg also knew the secrets of the world, but, as befits a good wife, she kept silent about them.

Odin, the All-father

WHEN Odin sat on the Lidskjalf, two fierce wolves lay at his feet and two black ravens perched on his shoulders. At dawn he would send the ravens off to fly over the world and look into the darkest corners. At noontime they would come back to sit on his shoulders and whisper into his ears all the secret things they had learned. Nothing was hidden from Odin, the raven god, when he sat on the Lidskjalf.

When Odin peered into the farthest reach of Jotunheim, he could see a gigantic eagle sitting at the northern edge of the world. The eagle was really a jotun in disguise, and he was the maker of storm winds. When he lifted his huge wings the north winds blew out from under them, and when he flapped them, icy storms howled over the world. As the bitter blasts swept through the bleak halls in Jotunheim, the jotuns broke out of their icebound realm and rushed against the earth, pelting the valleys with snow and rolling blocks of ice down from the mountains. For the wild jotuns hated men as much as they hated the Aesir, and always tried to destroy them.

But Odin saw one jotun named Mimir, who was wise and not wild. He was the owner of a magic spring that welled up where one of Yggdrasil's roots ended in Jotunheim. It was the Well of Wisdom. In it lay hidden all the knowledge of the age-old race of the jotuns, and Mimir, who quenched his thirst at the well each morning, was the wisest of the wise.

Odin went to Mimir and asked if he too might drink from his well. Mimir was too wise to hate the Aesir, but he would let him drink only if, in return, Odin would share his all-seeing sight. So Odin gave his left eye to Mimir and drank. After that Odin was the wisest of the wise, for he had the wisdom of both jotuns and Aesir. Of course, he was one-eyed now and so he always kept half of his face hidden by a wide-brimmed hat or a strand of his hair. But his remaining eye gleamed brighter than ever.

Mimir hid Odin's eye deep in the Well of Wisdom, and when he looked down through it, he could see everything in the wide world. From then on, he was Odin's great friend and adviser.

Thor, the Thunder-god

STRONGEST of the Aesir was Odin's son Thor, the god of thunder. His temper was as fiery as his bristling red beard; he struck out before thinking, and his blows were not soft.

He had a magic hammer, the Mjolnir, which smashed to bits whatever it struck. He also had an iron mitt and a magic belt; when he put on his belt his enormous strength was doubled.

The mere mention of jotuns and trolls made Thor furious, and whenever he heard that some of them had broken out of their icebound realm, he flew into a rage. He would dash off to fight them in his cart, which was drawn by two billy goats so wild they gnashed their teeth. Lightning flashed from their hoofs, and the wheels of the cart thundered over the leaden clouds. Thor would throw his hammer from afar, and it would hurtle through the air and crush the stony head of a jotun. Then, it would fly back to Thor to be thrown again and again. It was red hot, but Thor could catch it with his iron mitt.

At home on Asgard, Thor was kind and good-natured. He was very proud of his two sons, Magni and Modi, who were almost as strong as he was, and he adored his golden-haired wife, Sif. He loved to give big and noisy feasts in his hall, which was enormous. Room opened upon room—altogether there were five hundred forty of them. There, by the "long fires" his guests gorged themselves with food and drink. Thor was a glutton himself, and he thought nothing of eating a whole roast ox and a couple of salmon, and washing it all down with kegs of sweet mead.

The Aesir depended greatly on Thor. They had only to call his name and there he was, no matter how far away he had been. The Aesir called him often. Without him the jotuns might well have won over them.

Loki, the God of the Jotun Race

WHEN ODIN was still young—before he had hanged himself on Yggdrasil and drunk from the Well of Wisdom—his eyes had fallen on a jotun named Loki. He was graceful and handsome, not uncouth and misshapen like most of his race. Many jotuns could change themselves into wolves or eagles, but Loki could take on any shape he wished, even female ones. Nimble-witted and bright, full of clever ideas, Loki was like a flickering, shining flame, and Odin was so taken with him that he asked him to be his blood brother. Loki gladly accepted the offer. So each cut a small vein in his arm and, letting their blood flow together, they solemnly swore to be as true brothers from then on. They would stand by each other, defend each other, and never accept a favor unless it was also offered to the other.

Thus Loki, the jotun, became one of the Aesir and moved up to Asgard, where the great and holy ones welcomed him. Thor especially liked to have cunning Loki at his side, for Thor was not quite as quick-thinking as he was fast-acting. Loki helped him out of many a scrape, but he also got him into some.

Odin gave Loki one of the goddesses, Sigunn, for his wife. She was loving and kind and very patient with her fickle husband. But in Jotunheim, Loki had another wife, the dreadful ogress Angerboda. She was a better match for him, for, as the Aesir soon found out, Loki was really vicious and spiteful. He loved to play mean tricks, and it didn't matter to him whom he tricked. Neither Aesir nor jotuns could trust him, and he was always causing trouble.

But Loki was so quick-witted and honey-tongued that the Aesir always forgave him his misdeeds. Besides, Odin's blood flowed in his veins and no one dared to harm him.

Sif's Golden Hair

FORTUNATELY for the Aesir, Loki's mean jokes sometimes came back on his own head. Neither Odin nor Thor would have been so powerful had it not been for the dreadful thing Loki did to Sif, Thor's wife. All of the goddesses were lovely, but none had hair as beautiful and golden as Sif. Her hair gleamed as brightly as a field of ripe barley when lightning flashed over it, and, indeed, it was she who made the seeds ripen to golden grain after Thor's thundershowers had made them sprout.

Great was Thor's horror when he woke up one morning and saw a cropped head next to his! During the night someone had sneaked in and had cut off all of Sif's beautiful hair. There was nothing worse for a

woman than the shame of a bald head, and only Loki could have done such an awful deed. In a fury so wild that sparks flew from his beard, Thor stormed at Loki, threatening to break every bone in his body.

"Spare me," cried Loki, "and I promise that I will make the gnomes forge new hair for Sif, and that of real gold."

Thor let him go, and Loki ran off. He rushed deep underground to the sons of the gnome Ivaldi, who were famous for their fine work. Like all gnomes, they were ornery and cross and hated to do favors for anyone, but Loki knew how to sweeten their ill-humor with flattery, and before long they promised to do whatever he wished.

"Make the Aesir marvel," cried Loki. "Use all your magic powers and all your skill as smiths, and forge a head of golden hair that will grow on Sif's head like real hair. Then fashion a sharp spear that will never miss its goal, and if you can do it, make a ship that can sail over land and sea." Loki knew that all the Aesir were really angry and that he must bring more than Sif's new hair to be forgiven.

The sons of Ivaldi went to work. They drew magic circles, they laid spells, they mumbled incantations, and they spun hair for Sif out of gold. With equal skill they forged a magic spear and a flying ship made from thousands of tiny slats. Loki's laughter crackled like the fire in the gnomes' forge as he ran up to Asgard with the gifts.

As Loki had expected, Thor's angry face lit up when he saw the golden hair take root and grow as soon as he put it on Sif's bare head. It was even more gleaming and golden than her own hair had been.

Loki gave the spear to Odin, who called it the Gungnir. Odin was very pleased to have a spear that could not miss its goal, and all the Aesir admired it.

But the ship was the most wonderful. The gnomes had forged it so skillfully, of so many little pieces, that it could fold up to fit into a pouch. Still, it could be big enough to carry all the Aesir and all their gear. And the ship, the Skidbladnir, was so wrought with magic that the winds were always ready to change and fill its sail.

Of course, having these marvelous gifts, the Aesir forgave Loki. They even praised him for getting such fine work out of the grumpy gnomes. And Loki strutted about bragging loudly that no smiths in the world could equal his friends, the sons of the gnome Ivaldi.

A gnome named Brokk heard his words. He was outraged, for he was sure that his brother Sindri was the finest of all smiths. Brokk rushed up to Loki screeching angrily, "I will bet my head against yours that my brother Sindri can forge more wonderful things."

Loki readily accepted this bet, and Brokk hurried to his brother's smithy, deep underground.

"Brother Sindri," he moaned, "I have bet my head against Loki's that you are the best smith in the world."

"That I am," said his brother, "and you will not lose your head as long as you can keep the bellows going with both hands so that the fire in the forge is red hot. In the meanwhile I shall use my skill and draw my magic circles. Then we shall see what happens."

With that Sindri put a lump of gold and a pigskin on the forge. Warning Brokk to keep the fire red hot, he left to do his magic work

behind closed doors. Brokk busily worked the bellows until Sindri came back, although a fly that was buzzing around his ears bothered him greatly.

"Good work, Brother," said Sindri, and out of the fire he pulled a boar with golden bristles that shone brighter than the sunbeams.

"Ho," said Sindri, "here is a gift fit for a god! Keep the fires hot, brother." He put a lump of gold on the forge and left again.

Brokk worked the bellows, but the bothersome fly was back. This time it stung him upon his neck so hard that he almost had to let go of the bellows to whisk the fly away. Then Sindri came back, and he pulled a golden arm ring, a marvelous bracelet, out of the fire.

"Ho," said Sindri when he saw it, "this is really a gift for a god, for the king of kings. He who owns this arm ring will always have a gift to bestow upon his heroes, for every ninth night eight bracelets, as heavy and rich as the first, will drop from it."

"Now, Brother, whatever happens, keep the fire hot," said Sindri, and this time he put a lump of iron on the forge and left.

Again the fly came buzzing, and now it settled between Brokk's beetle brows and stung him so hard that blood trickled into his eyes. For a second he had to stop pumping the bellows to wipe away the blood. Sindri rushed in. "Brother," he wailed, "why did you let go of the bellows? Now you are lost!"

But when Sindri looked into the fire his face brightened. "Oh, it isn't so bad after all," he said. "I wanted to make a thunderbolt hammer, stronger than anything in the world. The head is perfect, the handle a bit short, but it will do in the proper hand." And he pulled a red-hot hammer out of the forge. It was Mjolnir, the thunderbolt.

When the bothersome fly saw the hammer, he took off at once; of course the fly was Loki in disguise, trying to spoil Sindri's work.

Brokk hurried up to Asgard with the treasures his brother had wrought, and the Aesir marveled when they saw them.

That was how Odin got his priceless arm ring, the Draupnir. To Frey went the golden boar, which shone like the sun when he rode it through the summer sky. To Thor went the magic hammer, the Mjolnir, which broke whatever it hit, and never got lost, for it always flew back to Thor's hand. It did not bother Thor that the handle of the red-hot hammer was a bit short, for his iron mitt kept his hand from being burned.

The Aesir judged the Mjolnir the greatest of all marvels. Brokk had won the bet and was free to take Loki's head. Loki tried to slip away, but Thor went after him, caught him in his firm grip, and brought him back. As Brokk drew his sword to cut off his head, Loki cried out, "Wait a bit, Brokk, I bet my head only and so you have no right to touch my neck."

The Aesir had to agree—he had bet only his head, and, as there was no way for Brokk to take it without touching his neck, Loki kept his head. However, he did not get away unpunished, for Brokk clamped his head with one strong arm and sewed up his mouth with a leather thong. Loki could not say one word, and nobody would undo the stitches for him. At last he tore his mouth open so hard that the thong broke, but for a long while he had a very sore mouth.

Loki's Monstrous Brood

ONE DAY as Odin sat on his throne, the Lidskjalf, looking into Jotunheim, what should he see but Loki playing with three young monsters. One was a spitting serpent, the second a snapping wolf, and the third was shaped like a hag but was pale as death on one side, black as peat on the other. They were the children of Loki and the dreadful ogress Angerboda.

"The father is bad, the mother is worse," said Odin in disgust. "No good can ever come from the offspring of such parents."

At once he summoned Loki and his brood to Asgard. Odin felt that one day these three monsters would bring disaster to the world, but as they were the offspring of his blood brother Loki, he could not kill them. He could only put them where they would do the least harm. So he flung the serpent into the ocean. It sank to the bottom and grew and grew until it lay in a circle around Midgard, the earth, with its fangs biting into its own tail. It was called the Midgard's Serpent.

The hag Odin sent deep underground to live on the doorstep of Niflheim and rule over the dead. Her name was Hel, and her realm was named for her. Gravely she welcomed all who had died of sickness or old age, but she did nothing to make her guests happy in her vast hall. The walls of the hall were a wickerwork of winding serpents; on the roof sat a soot-black cock who never crowed but was silent as death. Pitfall her doorstep was called, sickbed was the name of her lair, her knife was called hunger, her platter starvation. A high fence surrounded her realm, and her howling hound, Garm, stood chained to the gate. Once in a while she left her gate open, and then the dead people roamed all over the earth, to the horror of the living.

Beyond Hel lay Niflheim, a still grimmer place where those who had been really wicked were thrown. The most terrible spot in all of Niflheim was a whirlpool where the dreadful dragon Nidhogg lay chewing at the deepest root of Yggdrasil, the world tree.

Fenris, the wolf, the third of Loki's monstrous offspring, was dragged to an island in the middle of a lake surrounded by a forest of iron trees.

There he grew and grew and became so wild that Odin decided to have him chained to make sure he could not escape. But the huge wolf had grown so strong that all the Aesir together could not hold him by force; they had to cajole him to get the chain around him. They told him it was only a sport to test his strength and to see how fast he could free himself. Proud of his strength, Fenris agreed, and when the chains were put around him, he merely strained a bit and shook himself, and the iron links flew to all sides. Nothing but a magic bond could keep the monster tied up, so the Aesir enlisted the help of the gnomes. For once the gnomes were willing enough, because they too were afraid of the fearful wolf. They spell-caught the sounds of cat paws, the breath of fish, the spittle of birds, the hairs of a woman's beard, and the roots of a mountain, and spun them around the sinews of a bear. That made a bond that looked as fine as a ribbon of silk, but, since it was made of things not in this world, it was so strong nothing in the world could break it.

The Aesir took the bond and went out to the island again. At first Fenris refused to let himself be tied; he wasn't that stupid, but he was very vain. The Aesir played on his vanity.

"This bond is so much stronger than it looks that none of us can break it," they said. "Come, let us tie you with it to see how well you can do. If you can break it you will win great fame, and if you can't we give you our word that we shall untie you."

"I might let you tie me, but only if one of you will put his hand between my jaws to show your good faith," growled Fenris.

The Aesir looked at one another and at the wolf's gruesome fangs. Then Odin's son Tyr, bravest of them all, stepped forward and calmly put his hand between the frothing jaws. Quickly the Aesir threw the magic bond around Fenris's legs and fastened the ends to a rock deep underground. The wolf howled and growled and threw himself this way and that, but the more he tore at the bond, the stronger it became. When the Aesir saw that he could not get loose, they said, "Lie there and strain at your fetters till the world comes to an end," and left. Although they had broken their promise, they were all quite happy about the outcome, except for Tyr. He had lost his hand.

The wolf howled dismally, and the slaver ran from his jaws like a river. There he had to lie, but he grew and grew, because every day an old ogress came out from the forest of iron trees and fed him.

Balder, the God of Light

IT BOTHERED Odin greatly that the Aesir had broken their promise to Fenris, for a god must never break his word. But the monstrous wolf could not be left free as a threat to gods and men. He turned for comfort to his son Balder, who had not taken part in the deceit.

The Aesir always turned to Balder when they were troubled, for he was the kindest and gentlest of gods. No one could think anything but pure thoughts in his presence. Flowers sprang up from the ground wherever he stepped, but even the whitest and most beautiful of them, the Balderblom, was not as fair as his brow. Everybody loved him; not even the spiteful gnomes and uncouth jotuns could dislike Balder.

The light from his shimmering hall shone into the farthest corners of the world, and it was there that he sat in judgment on his golden throne. He never took sides, and was so kind he could not bear to mete out punishment. Although the Aesir brought their disputes to Balder, they seldom followed his advice. It was too gentle and forgiving.

Balder lived in great happiness with his loving wife Nanna and their son Forsete. Forsete was as constant as Nanna, his mother, and as just as his father, Balder. Calmly he studied the laws of the world and laid down judgments according to them, and his rulings always held. He became the chief judge of the Aesir.

Heimdall, the Watchman of Asgard

HEIMDALL, another of Odin's great sons, was the watchman for the Aesir. Early in the beginning of time, he had been born by nine sisters, nine lovely jotun maidens. Having so many beautiful mothers, he was wonderfully handsome; and he had a truly dazzling smile, for his teeth were of pure gold.

Heimdall was an excellent watchman. His clear blue eyes were so keen that he could see to the end of the world. So sharp were his ears that he could hear everything, even the sound of the wool growing on the sheep down on Midgard. And he needed no more sleep than a bird.

Odin had given him a trumpet-horn, the Gjallarhorn, to blow whenever he saw danger approaching. The sound of this horn was so loud that it could be heard shrilling over the whole wide world. Straight as a ramrod, with the Gjallarhorn at his side, Heimdall stood at the landing of the rainbow bridge, watching and listening so that no enemy could sneak into Asgard.

It happened one day that a woman dressed in glimmering gold came walking up the rainbow. The smoldering fire in the rainbow did not burn her feet, and Heimdall did not blow his horn. He only stared at her, for she was bewitchingly beautiful, and he did not stop her from entering Asgard.

All the Aesir flocked around her and admired her. She was Gullveig, and she had come from the world of the Vanir gods, the faraway world of the singing winds. Beautiful as Gullveig was, she really was a wicked witch. She had come to Asgard because she wanted gold, and the Aesir had plenty of it.

In no time at all the Aesir had begun to quarrel among themselves, each one trying to bring the most gold to Gullveig. Odin saw that she had brought evil into his peaceful home, and he angrily stood up and declared that Gullveig was a witch who must be burned.

She was put to the stake. Three times the fire was lit and three times she rose from the flames in a different shape. Her lust for gold burned hotter than the flames.

Njord, Frey and Freya

THE VANIR were peaceful gods, who ruled mild winds and gentle rains, but when they heard of Gullveig's mistreatment they grew very angry. The witch had, after all, come from their realm, and she had to be avenged. So they armed themselves and stormed up the rainbow.

Warned by Heimdall, the Aesir rushed out from their halls to stop the attackers. But the Vanir breeched the fence around Asgard and lined themselves up into battle formation on the great and sacred field of Ida. There the first battle fought in the world took place. It was fierce but evenly matched, and when the Aesir and the Vanir saw that neither of them could win, they agreed to put down their weapons. To ensure a lasting peace, they gave each other hostages. Odin sent his brother Hoenir to the world of the Vanir. He was a very handsome god, long-legged and swift of foot. But he was also a bit slow of thought and speech, so Odin persuaded Mimir, the wise and ancient jotun, to go with him as his adviser.

The Vanir gods were so taken in by Hoenir's stately appearance that they made him their chieftain. But as time went on, they found that he could not make a single decision without asking Mimir. They thought the Aesir had cheated them by sending someone stupid and unimportant as a hostage and this made them angry.

They did not dare harm Odin's brother, but they wanted revenge, so they cut off Mimir's head and sent it back to Asgard. Odin felt very unhappy about it and sent word to the Vanir that he had acted in good faith—Hoenir, one of the oldest of the Aesir, and Mimir, the wise old jotun, were the best he could give them for hostages. Then he used his magic powers and blew life back into Mimir's head. Ever after, in times of distress, he went to Mimir's head for counsel.

Hoenir stayed with the Vanir and there were no more quarrels between the Aesir and the Vanir.

The Aesir, for their part, were delighted with the hostages that came to Asgard. The Vanir had sent their god Njord and his two children, Frey and Freya.

Njord, who was very stately in appearance, was a good and fruitful god. He wove gentle winds to fill the sails of ships and he blew out wild fires. The Aesir gave him a sparkling hall with a shipyard by the shore of the celestial sea.

Frey was god of fertility. He sent life-giving showers and sunshine to earth and brought rich harvests with him. He had a sword which gleamed

as brightly as the sun and a horse which could dash through roaring flames, and the Aesir gave him the ship that could fly over land and sea and the marvelous golden boar that the gnomes had made. When Frey rode the boar across the summer sky, its golden bristles, shining like sun rays, lit up the darkest valleys, increasing manyfold the crops on earth. The Aesir gave Frey a palace in Alfheim, and the elves waited upon him.

Freya, Frey's sister, was the goddess of love. She came to Asgard in a carriage drawn by gray cats with her little daughter Noss on her lap. Noss was so sweet that her name was used to describe anything really delightful.

Freya, most beautiful of all the goddesses, was often sad, for her husband Od had disappeared. He was a wanderer and a dreamer and had been lost in one world or another. Freya often went looking for him. Sometimes she drove off with her cats and sometimes she flew off as a

falcon, for she had a suit of falcon feathers which carried her swiftly through the air when she put it on.

The Aesir built a hall for Freya in Asgard which was almost as big as Odin's. It had to be so big because Freya was very fond of company, and her hall was always thronged with merry men.

Still, Freya would often think of her lost husband and weep herself to sleep. But she was lovely even when she wept, for her tears, rolling silently down her round cheeks, were pure drops of gold.

Bragi, God of Poetry

WHEN the matter of the hostages had been settled, the Aesir and the Vanir sealed their pact of peace in a strange way. They gathered around a huge vat, chewed certain berries, and solemnly spat the juices into the vat. These divine juices took shape, and out of the vat rose Kvasir, the spirit of knowledge. There was no question that he could not answer, and no matter how much he was pumped for information, he never ran dry. On the contrary, his knowledge increased.

But one day, two gnomes drowned Kvasir in the essence of his own knowledge. Then they ran off with the essence to their home deep underground. There they poured it into three kettles, added honey, and sprinkled it with magic herbs. They brewed a mead so potent that whoever drank of it felt his spirit soar high and free, and ringing verse poured from his lips.

The mead made the gnomes feel so grand that they recklessly killed an old jotun, and when his wife came looking for him, they slew her too. But Suttung, the son of the old jotun couple, found out about it and came to avenge his parents. The gnomes could save their lives only by giving him the magic mead. Suttung hid the three kettles in a chamber deep in a mountain and set his daughter Gunnlod to watch over them.

From his throne, the Lidskjalf, Odin saw the jotun hide the three kettles and he decided that he must have the mead. So he changed himself into a snake and wormed his way into the mountain through a crack in the rock. When he came to the chamber where Gunnlod sat watching the mead, he took on the shape of a handsome young man.

"How sweet, how beautiful you are, sitting here deep in the mountain by your lonely self," he said. And indeed it was true. Gunnlod was one of the beautiful jotun maidens, and in her loneliness she liked hearing about it. So she smiled and enjoyed the company of her handsome young guest. After three days she had grown so fond of him that she said

he might have a sip from each of the three precious kettles she was guarding—one sip from each.

In three mighty gulps Odin emptied all three of the kettles; then he rapidly changed himself into an eagle and flew off. Poor Gunnlod sat weeping beside her empty kettles.

But Suttung, her father, saw the eagle fly away from the mountain, and right away he became suspicious. He also took on the shape of an eagle and set off in pursuit. And as Odin had three great kettlefuls of mead inside him, Suttung could fly faster.

Heimdall spied the two birds approaching Asgard and saw that the distance between them was becoming smaller and smaller. He knew what Odin had gone for, and he called to the other Aesir and told them to hurry and set all their pots and kettles out into the courtyard. Odin just barely had time to spit the mead into the vessels and fly to safety, so close upon his heels was Suttung. Thus Suttung had to return without his mead, and Odin kept it for himself.

After that Odin always spoke in stately verse. He let the other Aesir taste the magic brew, and he gave some to truly gifted men on earth. They became great poets, a joy to gods and men.

Odin had also lost some drops outside the wall of Asgard, and these dripped down to the earth, free for any fool to gather. But the drops had lost their magic power, and those who gathered them could write nothing but doggerel.

In this roundabout way poetry came into the world, to lift the hearts of Aesir and men. But Odin felt it always weighing on him that, to gain the gift of poetry, he had betrayed Gunnlod, a trusting maiden, and had left her alone to weep over her empty kettles.

To make up for it, Odin brought Gunnlod's son, Bragi, to Asgard. He recognized Bragi as his son, taught him the power of the runes, and gave him some of Suttung's mead to drink.

Thus Bragi became the god of the bards. And as a bard needs youth to sing, Odin gave him for his wife Idunn, the keeper of the apples of youth. Whoever took a bite from her apples did not grow old, and the Aesir depended upon Idunn and her apples to stay young.

With Idunn tenderly caring for him, Bragi always had sparkling eyes and rosy cheeks, although his face was framed by the long white beard of a sage.

Odin's Eight-legged Steed

WHEN the Vanir had attacked the Aesir, the silver and gold fence around Asgard had been breached, and the jotuns could now shoot their arrows of ice right into the green fields of Ida. So the Aesir gathered at the foot of Yggdrasil to consider the matter. After much talk they decided that a wall of stone must be built, turning Asgard into a real stronghold.

Just then a huge hulk of a man came driving along in a cart pulled by a great black horse. He would be glad to build the wall for them, he said, for he was a mason. The Aesir were delighted. They all loved to build with bricks of gold and shingles of silver, but to build a fortress wall of stone was a dreary chore, not a fitting task for gods. When they asked what the mason would want for payment, however, they were shocked. He wanted Freya herself, and also the sun and the moon!

"Preposterous!" they all cried. "We would never think of giving Freya to a stranger, and we would never rip the sun and the moon out of the sky, leaving the world in total darkness!"

They were just going to chase the mason away when Loki whispered, "Tell him you will give him what he asks, but on two conditions: he alone must build the wall, and he must build it within the span of a winter. Nobody can possibly build that wall in such a short time."

The Aesir listened to Loki's advice, and when the mason accepted the conditions they thought his arms must be much stronger than his wits, and they exchanged sly glances. They would have most of the stone wall built for nothing. What a cunning fellow Loki really was!

But as the winter went slowly by and a high wall rose and grew around them, the Aesir began to worry. Never had they seen a worker like the mason. He never slept, he never rested. All night long his huge black horse carted boulders as big as mountains up to Asgard. All day long, while the horse ate, the mason easily fitted the boulders into place. At last, with three days of winter still to go, only the gateposts were unfinished. The Aesir's worry turned to despair; they rushed at Loki and shouted:

"Traitor! You talked us into this with your slippery tongue. Now you get us out of it!" And they seized him by the neck and shook him. "We cannot give beautiful Freya to an unknown stranger and plunge the world into darkness. Now *do* something!"

The frightened Loki begged, "Please let go of my neck and I promise I will find a way out." So the Aesir let him go, and Loki scampered into the woods.

That evening, when the mason came driving his horse down through the woods to start his night's work of hauling stones, a sleek young mare ran out in front of his cart. She neighed softly, tossed her head, kicked high her heels, and trotted back into the woods.

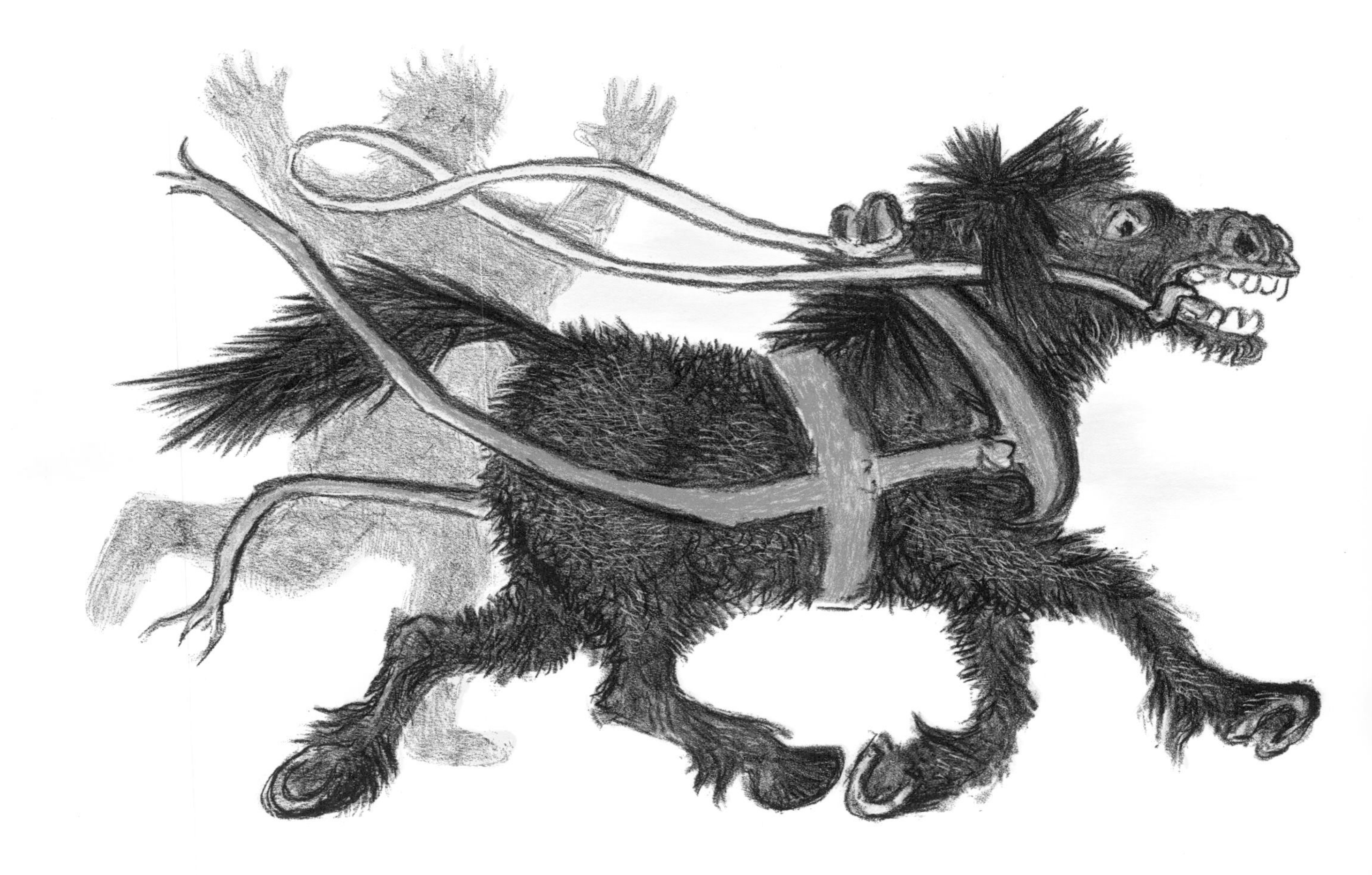

The mason's big black stallion bolted and tore off after the mare. The mason ran after his horse.

Late the next day he caught up with him, but both mason and horse were too exhausted to do any carting and building of stone walls. So the wall was still unfinished when winter came to an end.

Then the mason realized that he had been tricked, and, showing his true nature, flew into a jotun rage. For he really was a jotun disguised as a mason. With all his great strength he began to tear down the wall he had built, threatening to destroy whoever came near him.

When the Aesir saw that instead of a stupid mason they had a raging jotun among them, they shouted for Thor.

Thor was away, chasing trolls, but the moment his name was mentioned he appeared; and when he saw that there was a jotun in Asgard, he did not think twice but threw his hammer that never missed. That was the reward of the jotun who tried to outwit the Aesir and carry

away Freya and the lights of the world.

The strong stone wall around Asgard was almost built, and the Aesir themselves easily finished what was left to do. They were pleased with themselves, and only Odin worried that the Aesir had again broken faith. The mason would have kept his part of the bargain, and the Aesir had not kept theirs.

The wall itself was good and strong, and nobody blamed Loki for his part. Still, for a long while he was not seen. Then one day he walked out of the woods leading a colt—a little gray colt that glided along on eight legs! The mare of course had been none other than Loki, and he had mothered the handsome colt.

In time the colt grew into a wonderful horse that no other horse could match. His eight legs were so swift that he ran like a storm wind through the air and over the billowing sea. Odin made him his personal steed and named him Sleipnir, the Glider.

The Valkyries and Valhalla

ODIN needed such a horse to take him like a storm wind from Asgard to battlefields on earth. There were many battlefields, for just as gods had fought in holy Asgard, men were fighting on earth. They fought each other for gold, they fought each other for land, they fought each other for the fun of fighting. And Odin was no longer only the great All-father and the wise wanderer; he was also the furious god of storm and war as well. Then he was called Ygg, the terrible one.

When he was seen in the gray light of dawn, racing his eight-legged steed over the towering clouds, people knew that somewhere a bloody battle would soon be fought. Both armies would be calling loudly to Odin, praying for the victory that he alone could give.

With his single eye flashing under a golden helmet and his huge body wrapped in a coat of mail, Odin would arrive at the battlefield. He would quickly decide who was to win, and then he would throw his spear, the Gungnir, over the host that must lose. He always tried to make the better warrior win, but sometimes it was a hard choice, especially when good men were fighting one another.

Odin was followed by a band of tall and handsome warrior maidens clad in shining armor, with winged helmets on their heads. As they stormed through the clouds their swords gleamed like lightning, and the foam from their panting steeds fell to the ground as hail. They were the Valkyries, Odin's maidens. Most of them were from Asgard, daughters of goddesses. But once in a while Odin was so taken by the brave spirit of a maiden on earth that he let her join the ranks of the Valkyries. They did not go to Asgard to live, but Odin gave them lovely white cloaks of swans' feathers so that they could fly around Midgard even when there were no battles raging. Proud was the hero who got a Valkyrie for a wife.

The Valkyries chose who would die in battle and brought the dead heroes up to Asgard. There they lived a life of glory in Odin's guesthouse, Valhalla. Odin foresaw that sooner or later a final battle between the Aesir gods and the forces of destruction would have to be fought, and he wanted a great army of good soldiers at his side.

And so it was that during a battle a warrior would feel a light tap on his shoulder. Turning, he would see a maiden with a winged helmet, and then he would know that he had been chosen as one of Odin's heroes.

With reckless fury, he would leap forward to bring down as many of the enemy as he could until he himself fell in battle. Then the Valkyrie would sweep his fallen body from the ground, throw him across her saddle, and ride with him to Asgard, while far down below the galloping hoofs of her horse the earth faded away.

In Asgard the horse would alight in a grove, where all the trees bore leaves of gold. The leaves would twinkle merrily as the Valkyrie led her hero up the well-trodden path to Valhalla. And, if the hero had acted with great valor, Odin himself would offer him a welcoming drink of sweet mead. Then the warrior would be led into the hall to take his seat among Odin's heroes and lead a life of riotous feasting and fighting.

Valhalla was the greatest of all buildings; it was so big that one could hardly see the opposite wall. Five hundred and forty doors could be flung open, each of them so enormously wide that almost a thousand men could march through side by side. Strong spears held up the roof, which was shingled with round shields. The walls of the hall were hung, not with soft tapestries, but with coats of mail and helmets. A long fire blazed down the middle of the hall, and on the benches that lined it on both sides, there was room for thousands upon thousands of Odin's heroes. There was never a lack of space for a newcomer in Valhalla.

The Valkyries rushed about, keeping the heroes' platters filled with food and their drinking horns overflowing with beer and sweet mead. There was no end to the heroes' eating and drinking.

A strange goat lived on the roof of Valhalla, grazing on the branches

of an overhanging tree. Instead of milk, mead flowed from her udder—so much mead that the kettles put out to catch it could barely be kept from overflowing, however heartily the heroes drank.

A great hog kept them well supplied with fresh meat. Every morning the hog was butchered, boiled, and devoured; at night it would be alive again, to be butchered the next morning and eaten again. Nothing tasted better to the tongues of dead heroes than fresh pork.

At the north wall of Valhalla was Odin's seat of honor, and there he sat when he came to feast with his heroes. Near him sat four of his sons, Tyr and Hod, Vidar and Vali, war gods all. Tyr ate with his left hand, since Fenris the wolf had bitten off his right hand. He was the bravest of the brave, and he urged men to war. Hod, who was very strong, was blind, and he led raging warriors into bloody battles.

When the feasting was over and Odin had retired, the heroes rolled over and went to sleep on benches strewn with fresh hay. In the morning the golden cock that perched on Valhalla's roof roused them with his crowing. The heroes woke up in a quarrelsome mood. They chewed toadstools to get themselves into a raging frenzy. Then, as wild Berserks, they jumped up from the benches, reaching for their coats of mail and weapons, and rushed out to fight one another on the field of Ida.

It was no sham battle—every hero fought furiously and soon the huge field was strewn with heads and limbs. But when the dinner bell rang, they all picked up their pieces, put them back where they belonged and streamed through the wide doors of Valhalla. There they settled down for another feast and once again were the best of friends.

Thus the heroes kept trim and fit and had a glorious time while they were at it.

Frigg and the Goddesses

IF ANY hero preferred gentle conversation and the company of women to feasting and fighting, he could go to Freya's hall, for Odin had given Freya permission to invite as many as half of the host to stay with her. Freya was a very busy hostess, for she not only looked after her own heroes, she also helped Odin entertain his heroes in Valhalla. So she did not have much time to spend with the other goddesses. They gathered around Frigg, Odin's favorite wife.

Frigg was first among the goddesses, and lived in a resplendent hall. She was forever spinning yarn with her golden distaff and spindle, while she kept an eye on the households down on earth. When she noticed that a housewife worked her loom hard and well, she might snip off a piece of her own yarn and send it down to her. No matter how hard the woman worked at her weaving, she could not use up the yarn given her by Frigg, for it never came to an end.

Three lovely young goddesses, Fulla, Gna, and Lin, were Frigg's special ladies-in-waiting. Lin watched over those men and women whom Frigg had singled out to protect from harm. Gna ran her errands down to earth, for Gna had a very swift horse. Fulla carried Frigg's chest and took care of her shoes, and Frigg kept no secrets from her.

The goddesses Eir and Var were also close to Frigg. Eir, the forebearing, was the goddess of healing, and all who were sick and suffering turned to her. Var, the true one, listened to the vows men and women made to each other, and punished those who broke them.

Frigg and the other goddesses were kept busy with their own duties. They rarely mixed into their husbands' doings, though they guided them

FULLA
GNA
LIN
FRIGG
GEFJON
SAGA
SIGUNN
NANNA
SKADE
GERD
IDUNN
SIF

from behind the scenes. But once women sent up such fervent prayers to Frigg that she decided to give them a helping hand.

Far to the south two mighty peoples were making war upon each other, and Odin could not make up his mind which valiant host deserved to win. At nightfall the warriors hushed their war cries and put down their weapons. Then Odin decided to give victory to the army he would see first when the sun rose in the morning. During the night all the women of one of the countries raised their arms and prayed to Frigg to help them and protect their households. Frigg was moved. She knew about Odin's decision, and she told the women what to do. Following her advice, they put on helmets and coats of arms. They drew their hair down to both sides of their faces and bound it under their chins, so that it looked as if they had beards. Then they gathered under the casement to the east, where Odin was apt to look out in the morning. As Frigg knew he would, Odin got out of bed, looked out, saw what looked to him like warriors with very long beards and asked, "Who are these long-beards?"

"The host you saw first in the morning, to whom you promised victory," Frigg answered.

Odin kept his promise and threw his spear over the other host. The husbands of the long-beards won, and the inhabitants of that country have been called the "Langobards" ever since.

Two goddesses, Saga and Gefjon, looked and acted so much like Frigg and were so often seen in Odin's company that many thought the three goddesses were one and the same.

Once Gefjon went with Odin to his favorite island, Fyn, in what is now Denmark. When she saw how delightful it was, Gefjon decided that she too would like to have a lovely green island like that. The sound was very wide, and there would be plenty of room for another blossoming island. So Gefjon disguised herself as a Midgard woman and went across the sound to the court of a king in what is now Sweden. She was a great storyteller, and was soon high in the king's favor. When she asked if he would give her the land she could plow around in a day and a night, he laughed and said yes.

Gefjon rushed north into Jotunheim, married a jotun, and had four enormously strong sons. She changed her sons into bulls, hurried them back, and hitched them to her plow. They pulled so hard and so quickly that sweat streamed from their glistening sides and made a dense fog rise

around them. The plow went so deep that the land was cut loose, and before morning came they had pulled it far out into the sound. The king was left with a big lake where the land had been. Gefjon fastened her new piece of land to a shoal, and that was the beginning of the beautiful island of Sjaelland, where Copenhagen is now.

Freya's Wonderful Necklace

ALL OF the goddesses wore beautiful jewelry, but Freya, the goddess of love and beauty, had the loveliest necklace in the world. It was made of gold and sparkling gems and glowed like red-hot fire. The gnomes had made it with great magic, and Freya was so fond of it that she never took it off.

Most of the Aesir loved to see the blazing jewel on Freya's snow-white bosom, but Loki's eyes flickered with greed whenever he looked at it. And one day he decided to steal it. That night, when all Asgard was asleep, he tiptoed to Freya's door, changed himself into a fly, and crept through the keyhole.

Freya lay asleep, dreaming about her lost husband, and tears of gold trickled down her cheek. She was beautiful, but Loki only had eyes for the jewel sparkling at her throat. He wanted to grab it, but even in her sleep Freya guarded it with her hand over the clasp. So Loki hummed and buzzed around her ear until at last Freya lifted her hand to shoo away the fly. In a flash Loki changed himself back into his own shape, and with fingers as long and thin as spiders' legs, lifted the necklace from Freya's throat. Then he silently sneaked away to the seashore, changed himself into a seal, and swam toward a rocky islet with the jewel in his mouth.

But Heimdall, who was faithfully standing guard at the rainbow landing, heard the splash as Loki dove into the water. Turning, he caught sight of something gleaming in the mouth of a seal, and that made him suspicious. He changed himself into a seal also and set off in pursuit. When Loki heard that he was being followed, he clambered quickly up onto the islet. He sat down on the jewel to hide it and looked around with innocent eyes as Heimdall came closer.

Heimdall was not fooled by all that innocence. He recognized Loki's eyes and understood that he had been up to no good. He threw himself at him, and barking, biting, beating their flippers, the two seals fought furiously. Heimdall was the bigger of the two, and at last he pushed Loki into the water. And there lay Freya's necklace, gleaming and blazing on the gray stone!

Heimdall returned the necklace to Freya, and Loki did not try to steal it again. But from then on Heimdall and Loki, who had never been friends, were deadly enemies.

Idunn's Apples of Youth

ONE DAY as Odin, Loki, and some of the Aesir were walking about down on the earth, they came to a valley where a herd of oxen were grazing. They were hungry, so they slaughtered an ox, built a fire, and started to cook it. The meat was cooking nicely when all of a sudden a gust of wind fanned the flames to one side. No matter what the Aesir did they could not keep the meat over the flames long enough to cook it. Then they heard a voice that said, "If you give me a share of the meat, I won't blow the flames away."

The Aesir looked down and all around. At last they looked up and saw a huge eagle sitting on the branch of a tree, beating his wings. Since they did not know that the eagle was really Tjasse, a storm jotun, they laughed and said, "Of course you can have your share." The gusts of wind stopped, and the meat was soon done to a turn.

But before the Aesir had tasted one morsel the eagle swooped down, grabbed all the tender pieces, and flew up onto the branch again. The Aesir jumped up angrily, and Loki, who had a very short temper, grabbed

a big stick of wood and struck the huge bird with all his might. The cudgel stuck as if glued to the bird, for the storm jotun cast a spell on it. And the other end stuck to Loki's hand. The eagle flew off, and Loki was dragged along behind, skimming the ground, bumping over stones and stumps. Try as he might, he could not get loose.

"I have you in my power," screeched the eagle. "I am the storm jotun Tjasse, and I won't let go of you until you vow to bring me Idunn and her apples of youth."

To save himself, Loki promised to do whatever was asked of him. Bruised and blue, he limped back to the other Aesir, who laughed at him, for they did not know what he had promised to do.

As soon as they returned home, Loki went to Idunn and said, "I saw the strangest apple tree down in the woods; it bore fruit that looked just like your apples of youth. Let me show you the tree, and bring your apples so you can compare them."

Idunn fell for the ruse. She had so few apples that she had to cut them into very small pieces to keep the Aesir from aging, and she was eager to find more. But no sooner had she and Loki come into the woods

than there was a mighty gust of wind and the storm jotun swept down, seized her and her apples, and flew off with her.

In vain did the Aesir search for Idunn, and as time went by, their youth began to fade away. Her husband, Bragi, the bard, lost all joy in his art; his sonorous voice turned weary and dull. The others tried to hide their wrinkles and graying hair, and even Freya's radiant beauty began to fade. Everyone needed a bite from Idunn's apples.

At last all the gods and goddesses gathered in council at the foot of Yggdrasil and asked one another when and where Idunn had last been seen. Then it came out that no one had seen her since she walked out through the gates of Asgard with Loki. So they seized Loki and threatened him with dreadful lingering pain if he did not confess where Idunn was. Loki trembled and begged to be spared and admitted that, to save himself, he had helped the storm jotun kidnap her.

"But please let me go and I will find Tjasse's hall and try to bring Idunn home with me," he said.

So the Aesir released him. Loki changed himself into a falcon and flew off, looking for the jotun's hall. He found it at last in the midst of stormy mountains. Fortunately the jotun and his men had gone fishing, and Idunn was alone in the hall. Rapidly Loki shrank Idunn and her apples into the shape of little seeds, put the seeds in a nutshell, put the nutshell into his beak, and flew off for Asgard.

When Tjasse came home he found Idunn gone, but he spied the falcon flying far away. He threw on his eagle's disguise and set off in pursuit. In a short time he was close behind Loki, for an eagle flies faster than a little falcon.

The Aesir, who were anxiously watching the race, saw that the eagle was about to catch Loki. They quickly piled wood shavings outside the wall of Asgard, and the moment Loki cleared it they lit the shavings. The fire flared skyward and Tjasse flew right into the flames. He fell to the ground and was destroyed.

Loki turned Idunn and her apples back into their true shape, and right away she gave all the Aesir and Asynjer a bite each from her precious apples. Freya regained her beauty, Odin his handsome manliness, Bragi his beautiful voice. In her kindness Idunn even gave a bite to Loki, and he became as sprightly and wicked as before.

Skade, the Ski-goddess

TJASSE had a daughter whose name was Skade. She was a wild and beautiful jotun maiden who spent most of her time skiing and hunting in her father's mountains. When Skade heard of Tjasse's death, she stormed up to Asgard, every bit as fierce and dangerous as a Valkyrie.

"My father's honor demands that you pay a fine for his death," she cried, for it was a rule in those days that a man's death must be paid for in gold or his name would be dishonored.

"You do have a claim on us," the Aesir agreed. "But since we know that your father left you a great pile of gold, perhaps you would rather have some other payment. We will give you the honor of choosing one of us as your husband, and that will make you one of the goddesses."

Skade said that that would satisfy her. But she did not want to seem too eager, so she made the condition that before she would choose a husband, the Aesir must make her laugh. And that, she thought grimly, would be a hard task for them; she was not in a laughing mood.

The Aesir accepted Skade's condition, but laid down a condition of their own. If they must make her laugh, then she must choose her husband by looking at their legs only. Skade agreed, and the Aesir set about the business of making her laugh.

But hard as they tried, she only wrinkled up her mouth. At last Loki had a billy goat brought up and tied himself to its beard. They both tugged and pulled with all their might. The billy goat bleated and

butted, and Loki screamed and kicked as they capered about. At last Loki made a somersault right into Skade's lap. Then she could not help it; she had to laugh. With that she had made peace with the Aesir, and it was time for her to choose a husband.

The Aesir lined themselves up, but before Skade was called they made a dense fog descend on them like a curtain so that she could see only their legs. Skade wanted Balder to be her husband, so as she looked up and down the handsome display of godly legs, she searched for his. She was sure that Balder, the handsomest of the Aesir, would be the only one with legs as perfect as her own. For Skade, the skier, had shapely and muscular legs.

At last she made her choice. Poor Skade—when the fog lifted, she saw that the legs belonged to Njord. But she would have to make the best of it even though she was very disappointed. Balder was happy, for he wanted no other wife than his faithful Nanna.

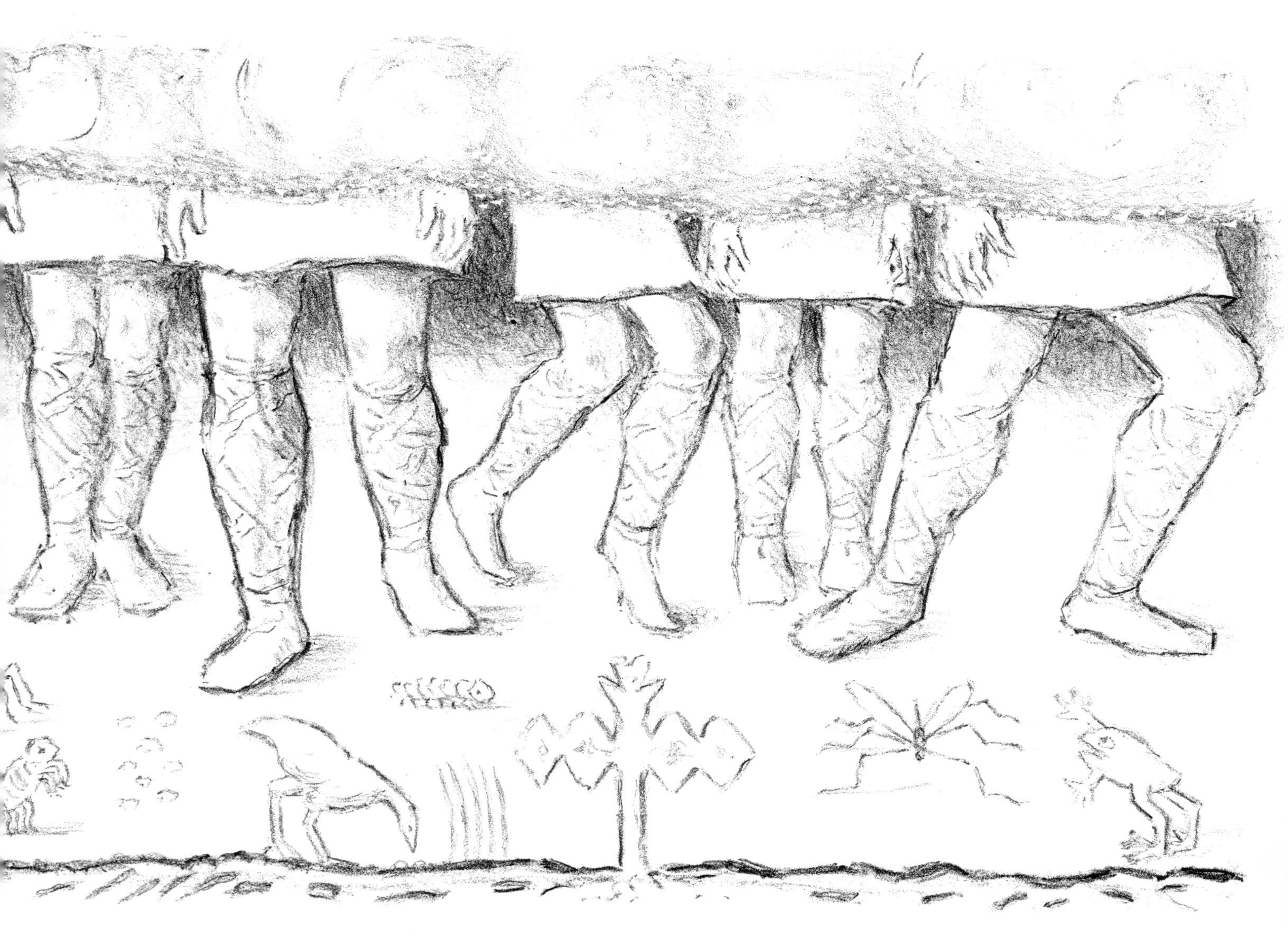

Skade and Njord were an ill-matched pair. He loved the seashore; she loved the mountains.

"It makes me sad to sit and stare at the wide open sea," she cried, "and the singing of the swans and the shrieking of the gulls pierce my ears and keep me awake all night."

After nine nights at Njord's home by the heavenly sea, they moved to Skade's hall in the mountains. Now Njord complained.

"The towering mountains shut me in," he sighed, "and the howls of the wolves keep me awake at night. I long for the song of the swans and the bright open sea."

After nine nights in the mountains, Njord moved back down to the sea.

Thereafter he and Skade seldom saw each other, but in a friendly fashion they went together to all godly gatherings.

Skade stayed in her mountains and became the goddess of skiers.

Ull, Thor's stepson, would have been a much better husband for her because he was the god of skiers. He hunted wild beasts and his skis

glided over the snowy mountains as swiftly as the arrows flew from his bow. No one, not even Skade, was his equal at skiing and hunting.

Frey and Gerd, the Jotun Maiden

LIKE HIS father Njord, Frey also married a jotun maiden, but this was the happiest of marriages. Frey knew very well that no one but Odin and Frigg should sit on Lidskjalf, the High Seat, but he often wondered how far they could see from it. So one day, when he saw it standing empty, he thought that surely no harm would be done if he mounted it and took a quick look.

As soon as he had seated himself, Frey looked into faraway Jotunheim and marveled at how well he could see even the littlest thing in that dusky world. Just then he saw a beautiful maiden walk across the courtyard of the jotun Gymir. As she lifted her snow-white arms to push open the door to the hall, a strange radiance spread from them and lit up the gloom of Jotunheim.

She was the most beautiful maiden Frey had ever seen, and he fell violently in love. He rose from the Lidskjalf and walked in a daze to Alfheim, his home. There he sat and mourned and grieved and could neither eat nor sleep. He knew that the maiden he loved was Gymir's daughter Gerd and that he had no hope of ever winning her, for her heart was as cold as a seed in frozen ground. Day and night Frey brooded and would not speak to anyone. He forgot to balance sunshine and rain, and he never heard the prayers of men whose tilled fields showed no life. He paid with sorrow for sitting where no one but Odin should sit.

His father and all the Aesir worried at seeing Frey pine away while the fields on earth lay barren; and they told Skirnir, his faithful servant, to sit at his master's feet and find out what was wrong. And to him, at last, Frey opened his heart.

"I love Gerd, the maiden with the frozen heart," he moaned. "I love her so much I do not think I can live without her. But custom forbids me from going myself, and I know that neither elves nor Aesir would ever take her my gifts and woo her for me. The maiden is cold and the trip is forbidding."

"I shall go to Jotunheim and woo Gerd for you," cried Skirnir, "but first you must give me your gleaming sword which strikes out by itself against jotuns and trolls, and you must also lend me your horse, which leaps through fire and flames."

"I will give them to you gladly," said Frey. "Only hurry and come back before I die of love for this maiden."

So Skirnir set off on the dangerous journey. Witches and many-headed trolls tried to stop him as he rode through dark and haunted valleys. Swinging Frey's sword, he made his way to Gymir's realm in Jotunheim. A wall of magic flames surrounded the realm, but he spurred his horse and it leapt through the flames. He came to the door of Gerd's chamber, across the courtyard from her father's great hall, and there he was stopped by a pack of snarling dogs.

Gerd sat in her chamber surrounded by her maidens. She heard the thumping of the horse's hoofs and the barking of the dogs. "Go out and see who has come to my door and bid the stranger welcome," she said to a little handmaiden. So the maid ran out and held the dogs at bay, and led Skirnir in to her mistress. Gerd bid him welcome with a cup of ice-cold mead and asked what errand had brought him.

"I have come for my master Frey, the giver of sunshine and life-giving rain. He asks you to give him your love," Skirnir answered. "If you will promise to be his bride, I will give you eleven gleaming and golden apples."

"Keep your apples," said Gerd. "I would rather grow old unwed than promise my love to Frey, the giver of sunshine and life-giving rain."

"I will give you this magic ring of gold if you will give your hand to Frey," Skirnir pleaded.

"In my father's house there is gold enough," said Gerd, tossing her proud head. "No one can buy my love with gold."

"Then I will cut off your proud head with one stroke of Frey's gleaming sword," cried Skirnir, and he sprang to his feet.

"Never will fear drive me to love," was Gerd's haughty answer.

In great anger Skirnir pulled out a stick, and on it he carved the rune ᚦ, a rune fraught with evil magic.

"Gerd," he chanted, "now I am casting a spell upon you. If you refuse to give Frey your love, no one but a three-headed troll with icicles dangling from his beard shall ever ask for your hand. Into a gray, old hag I will turn you and dry as a thistle you will be. You shall hide behind your fence and be a sight for all to see."

At that Gerd trembled and turned pale. "Undo your spell," she cried, "scratch out your evil rune, and I shall promise to give my love to Frey. Return to him and tell him that nine nights from now I shall meet him at Barre, the sacred barley patch."

Then Skirnir joyfully emptied the goblet of mead with which Gerd had greeted him, took his leave, and sped back to his master.

Frey was standing at his doorstep watching for him. "What has kept you so long?" he shouted before the horse had even stopped. "What news do you bring? Is it good? Is it bad?"

"I bring you good news," said Skirnir. "Nine nights from now Gerd will be yours."

"So long!" Frey sighed. "How can I wait for nine long nights?"

Nine lonesome days and nights seemed like nine months to Frey, but he survived, and at last his wedding day came. Gerd kept her word, and came to the sacred barley patch.

When Frey took her in his arms her cold heart melted. She turned into a warm and loving wife, and with that every frozen seed on earth burst its shell and came to life.

In this great happiness, Frey sent an abundance of sunshine and rain to the earth. The barren fields turned green once more and brought forth a richer harvest than ever before. And mankind blessed him and Gerd.

The Theft of Thor's Hammer

WHEN THOR woke up in the morning, the first thing he did was reach for his hammer. But one morning the hammer was gone! Thor jumped to his feet and tore at his hair and tugged at his beard and bellowed, "Loki, come here!" When Loki came, Thor whispered close to his ear, "My hammer has been stolen."

Loki turned pale. He knew that Thor's hammer must be found before the jotuns heard of its loss and gathered to attack Asgard. "Ask Freya to lend me her swift falcon wings and I will fly off and look for the thief," said Loki. He was in a trustworthy mood just then.

Together they rushed to Freya's hall. She also turned pale when she heard the terrible news. "I would gladly entrust my falcon wings to Loki, even if they were made of gold," she cried. "Only be quick and find Thor's hammer."

Like an arrow Loki flew off. When he came to Jotunheim, he saw the jotun Thrym sitting on a hillock, plaiting the manes of his mares with ribbons of gold. He was in a very merry mood, and when he saw Loki he greeted him politely. "How are the Aesir, how are the elves, and what might your errand be today?" he said, and made a show of good manners. Such smooth words from an uncouth jotun made Loki suspicious, but he returned the greeting just as politely and asked if Thrym by any chance might happen to know something about Thor's hammer.

"I stole it while he slept," the jotun said with a leer. "And what is more, I have hidden it eight miles underground. I will give it back to him, but only if Freya becomes my bride. I have plenty of gold, herds of black cows, and all these fine mares. The only thing I want that I do not have is beautiful Freya."

Swiftly Loki flew back to Asgard, where Thor and Freya were waiting for him.

"Hurry," he said to Freya, "put on your bridal veil. The jotun Thrym has Thor's hammer and he won't give it back unless you go to Jotunheim and take him for your husband."

"Never!" cried Freya, huffing and puffing so hard in her rage that her necklace broke and flew from her bosom. "Never shall it be said that Freya was so lovelorn she took a jotun for a husband!" At the mere thought, angry golden teardrops sprang from her eyes.

The other Aesir were now called in and the goddesses too. They all agreed that Freya must not marry a jotun, but that Thor must have his hammer back. They thought hard, and at last Heimdall spoke up.

"You must go yourself, Thor," he said. "You must wear Freya's wedding dress and play the blushing bride."

Thor protested loudly, but all in vain. The Aesir hid his sturdy legs beneath a trailing skirt, put a belt with dangling keys around his waist, and covered his chest with jewels and Freya's sparkling necklace. Then they tied his hair up in a topknot and hid his face behind the bridal veil. He was a dazzling bride.

"A bride needs a maid," said Loki. "I will be his maid."

So Loki was also dressed as a girl, Thor's goats were fetched, and off they went in Thor's cart, rumbling over the clouds.

Thrym heard them coming from afar and cried, "Quick, cover benches and floor with fresh straw and prepare my wedding feast. Thor has sent my bride."

They were seated at the table, and the feast began. Right away the bride ate all the sweets set aside for the women. Then she devoured eight salmon and finished the meal with a whole roasted steer.

Thrym gaped. "Never did I see such a gluttonous bride," he said.

"The poor girl has tasted nothing for eight long days," said Loki, the maid. "She has been pining away for you."

Hearing this, Thrym wanted to kiss her and lifted her veil. But when the eyes of his "bride" met his, he staggered halfway back across the hall as if struck by a thunderbolt. "Why do Freya's eyes glow as red as embers?" he gasped.

"That is because she hasn't slept for eight nights, longing for you," said Loki, the fast-thinking maid.

"Hurry!" cried Thrym, all aflame, "proceed with the wedding ceremonies. Bring up Thor's hammer and put it on Freya's lap, and let us make our vows of marriage."

The hammer was placed in the lap of the bride, who now sat modestly in her seat. Thor's heart laughed within him as his hand closed on the handle. He rose to his feet and wriggled his eyebrows. The veil fell down, and with flashing eyes he lifted his hammer and threw it. Thrym and all his kin came to a rapid end, smashed by the thunderbolt, and the great hall lay in rubble.

Thor and Loki jumped into the billy-goat cart and drove back to Asgard. Now that Thor held his hammer in his hand, they did not much mind the women's skirts about their knees. Thunder rumbled and lightning flashed, and all the Aesir drew a sigh of relief.

Thor and the Jotun Geirrod

ONCE when he had nothing better to do, Loki took on the shape of a falcon and flew off to see what he could see. He happened to fly over the hall of Geirrod, one of the strongest of the jotuns, and wondered what might be going on inside. So he glided down and perched on a window's ledge, high up under the eaves. Down in the hall he saw Geirrod sitting among his men, drinking and carousing by the fire, and boasting that he could easily conquer Asgard were it not for Thor and his hammer. As he raised his drinking horn to take another mighty swallow, he caught sight of the falcon up on the ledge.

"Bring me that bird," he roared to one of his men.

Loki snickered as he watched the man clambering and clawing his way up the high, slippery wall. But when it was time for him to fly away, he found that he could not move—the jotun had put a spell on him. So the man caught him and brought him down to Geirrod.

"This is no bird," the jotun said as he looked into Loki's eyes. "It is someone in disguise. Speak, tell me who you are." But Loki did not open his beak; he only stared back at the jotun.

"I'll teach you to talk," yelled Geirrod, and shut him up in a chest. There he kept him for three months with nothing to eat or drink; and when he took him out, Loki had grown so hungry and meek that he not only admitted who he was, he also promised to do whatever Geirrod wanted if only Geirrod would spare his life.

"I'll let you go," said the jotun with an evil grin, "if you will swear to bring Thor to me without his weapons."

Whimpering, Loki swore to do what the jotun asked and took off for Asgard as fast as he could. When he got home he gorged himself with food and drink; then, patting his stomach, he went to the glutton, Thor, and said, "I have just returned from Jotunheim, where I had quite a meal at Geirrod's hall. He brags loudly about his strength, but really, he isn't much of a jotun. I almost threw him in a friendly wrestling match before the meal, and you could throw him with your little finger. But he sets the finest table. You should have tasted the salmon and savory roasts and the foaming beer!"

So much did Loki talk about the food that Thor must have some too, and the end of it was that Thor set off with Loki for Geirrod's hall, leaving his weapons at home. For who, as Loki said, would believe that he came to Jotunheim on a friendly visit if he brought his hammer, his iron mitt, and his belt of strength?

On the way they stopped at the hall of the giantess Grid. She was the mother of Thor's half-brother Vidar, so she was friendly to the Aesir. When she heard that Loki and Thor, without weapons, were on their way to Geirrod's hall, she took Thor aside and said:

"Geirrod isn't a glutton at all, but a very strong and cunning jotun. Don't let yourself be fooled. Here, take my iron mitt and my magic belt and also my magic staff, and watch your step."

Thor thanked her, hid the belt and mitt under his coat, took the staff in his hand, and went on his way as if nothing had happened, with Loki at his side. But as they were fording a wide river, the water suddenly rose. Ramming Grid's staff down as hard as he could, Thor kept his feet from being swept away, and Loki hung onto him, while the river rose higher and higher. The water had almost reached his neck before Thor caught sight of a giantess straddling the river up above. It was she who made the river rise. Thor picked up a boulder from the bottom of the river and flung it at her, and the boulder did not miss its mark. Screaming, the giantess raced off. She was one of Geirrod's daughters who had been sent to drown them.

"Rivers must be stemmed at their source," said Thor.

Fortunately the branches of a rowan tree were hanging over the

river. Thor caught hold of one of the branches and hauled himself and Loki to safety and walked on.

When they arrived at Geirrod's, they were shown into a little house. It was furnished with only one stool but Thor was not choosy. He sat down on the stool, and as soon as he was seated, he felt the stool begin to move upward. Higher and higher he went, up toward the roof beam, and he saw that soon his head would be crushed. Then Thor put Grid's staff against the roof beam and pushed with all his might. And what with his own muscles and Grid's belt of strength, it was quite a push! The stool, with Thor on it, crashed down to the floor. There was a loud cry, and when Thor looked, there under the stool lay two of Geirrod's daughters, who had been lifting the stool. Their backs were broken, instead of his head.

"Now I know what kind of meal is waiting for me in Geirrod's hall," said Thor.

When the servants called him for dinner, he put Grid's iron mitt on his hand to be ready for his welcome and walked into the hall. Geirrod was standing by the fire with a pair of tongs in his hand. The moment he saw Thor he grabbed a red-hot iron bolt out of the embers and flung it at him. Thor caught it in his mitt and flung it back with all his might. The jotun ducked behind a pillar, but the glowing bolt flew through the pillar, through the jotun, through the wall of his hall and deep into the ground behind it.

"One evil jotun less is better than the grandest meal," said Thor, and he bore Loki no grudge. But he returned to Asgard with a greater appetite than ever.

Thor and the Jotun Utgardsloki

ONE DAY Thor decided to go and try his strength against an enormous fellow named Utgardsloki. He was the strongest of all the jotuns. He was also known to be the slyest of them all, so Thor asked Loki to come along. Utgardsloki's realm was far, far away, and they drove the whole day long in Thor's billy-goat cart. With a great rumble they stopped late at night at a little farm and asked for shelter. The farmer and his family were overcome by this great honor and scrambled about trying to scrape together enough food for Thor.

"Never mind; I have brought my own victuals," said Thor, and he butchered the goats, skinned them carefully and had the meat cooked. "Eat your fill," he told the farmer and his family, "but be careful not to crack a single bone. Put them neatly back on the skins when you have gnawed the meat off."

With that everyone fell to, and nobody noticed that the farmer's son Tjalfi cracked a shinbone on the sly and sucked the marrow. The next morning Thor swung his hammer over the skins and bones, and the goats jumped up as alive as ever, but one of them had a lame leg.

"Who has dared to crack a bone?" Thor shouted, and he lowered his brows in a scowl so dark that everyone but Loki trembled.

"Please don't kill us," the farmer begged. "As payment for the cracked bone, take my son Tjalfi for your servant. He is a hard worker and can run faster than the wind."

Thor accepted the offer, left his goats so the farmer could heal the injured one, and walked off, with Loki and Tjalfi following. At nightfall they came to a forest in Jotunheim with trees so tall their tops disappeared among the clouds. There wasn't a house in sight, and they did not like the thought of sleeping out in the open in Jotunheim, so they walked on. At last in the darkness they saw a very strange cabin that had neither smoke hole nor windows, and no front wall. But at least it would be a roof over their heads, so they went in, ate the food which Tjalfi had brought, and lay down to sleep.

In the middle of the night they were awakened by an earsplitting din. They jumped to their feet and groped around in the darkness until they found a little side room. There Loki and Tjalfi hid themselves

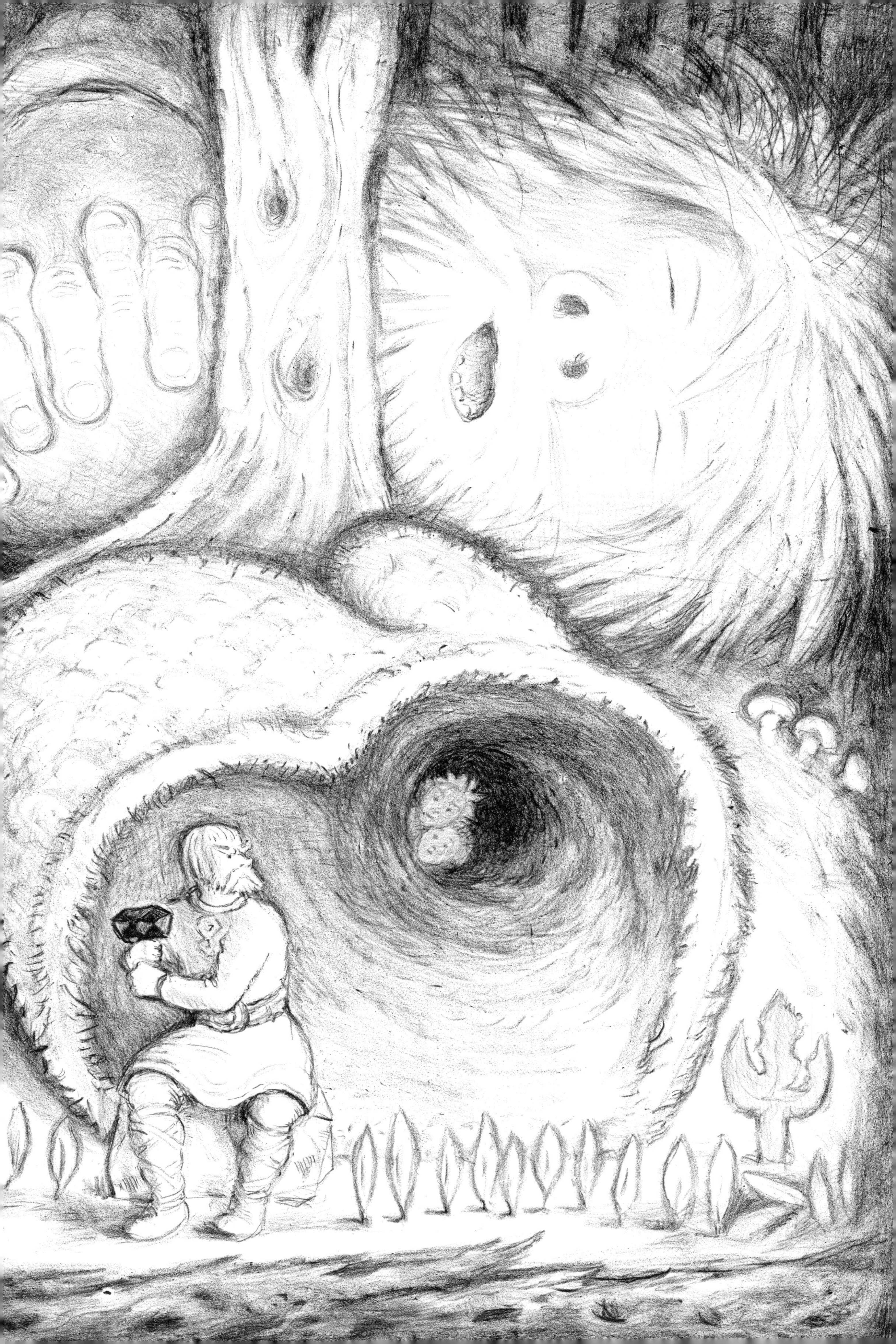

while Thor sat down outside to keep watch, hammer in hand

The whole night long there was such a growling and a snarling and a roaring that even Thor felt uneasy. When daylight came, at last, he saw a gigantic fellow lying on the ground fast asleep. From his wide-open mouth came a deafening snore—and that was the din which had kept them awake all night!

What they had taken for a cabin was one of the giant's mittens, and the little side room was the thumb! So huge was the giant that Thor hesitated to throw his hammer. Just then the enormous fellow woke up, yawned, stretched himself up to the treetops, and looked around.

"Well, well," he said. "That little runt down there with the hammer must be mighty Thor himself. They call me Skrymir," he added. Then he sat down, untied his huge bag of food, and began to eat a tremendous breakfast. He did not offer a morsel to Thor, who had to be content with the bit of food Tjalfi carried in his little bag.

When Skrymir had eaten his fill, he got up and proposed that they travel together. Since they seemed to be going the same way, they might as well keep together and share their food, he said.

Thor certainly had nothing against that, so the giant tied Tjalfi's little bag inside his big one, threw it over his shoulder and set off with mighty strides. Thor and his companions had to trot to keep up, and they were very hungry and tired when evening came. Skrymir threw his bag down and stretched out under a tree.

"There, eat," he said. "I am still full, so I am going to sleep." And he began to snore as loudly as he had the night before.

Thor and his companions threw themselves on the food bag. But as much as they tugged and pulled at the string, they could not undo the knot. At last it dawned on Thor that Skrymir was making fun of his famous strength. He shook with anger, grasped his hammer with both hands, stepped forward and gave Skrymir a mighty blow on his head.

Half in sleep, Skrymir mumbled, "Did a leaf fall on my head, or what? I hope you found food to your liking, Thor. But why aren't you asleep?" Then he snored again.

Well, Thor and his companions had to go to bed on empty stomachs. Tired as they were, though, they could not sleep, for Skrymir's snoring kept them awake. At last Thor jumped up, swung his hammer again, and brought it down on the giant's head with still greater force.

Skrymir muttered, "What was that? It must have been an acorn falling on my head. But why aren't you sleeping, Thor?" And soon he was snoring louder than ever.

Now Thor was boiling with rage. "I swear I will make an end to him," he said. Swinging his hammer round and round he brought it down on Skrymir's head with a terrific crash. This time Skrymir really woke up.

"Must have been a branch that hit me," he said, rubbing his head. "Well, it is time to get up anyway. I turn off here, Thor, but I have enjoyed your company so much that I will give you a friendly warning before I leave you. From your whispering I know you are going to Utgardsloki; take care. You thought I was good-sized, but he is taller than I, and he won't stand for any swaggering from an urchin like you." With that he slung his sack over his shoulder and was off, leaving Thor, for once, feeling rather small and weak.

Thor and his companions continued on their way, and at noon they came to a stronghold so big that they had to bend their heads way down

their backs to see the tops of its walls. The huge gate was locked, but they managed to squeeze through between the bars and walked across the courtyard to a vast hall. The door stood ajar, and inside they saw many huge jotuns sitting on two long benches facing the fire. The tallest of them sat in the middle and the shortest at the ends. Biggest of them all was Utgardsloki, and he was simply enormous.

Thor remembered Skrymir's warning, and he and his followers went up to Utgardsloki and greeted him politely. For a while the jotun did not seem to notice them, then he leaned forward and squinted at them.

"If I am not mistaken, that little fellow clutching a hammer must be Thor, the mighty thunderer himself," he said with a grin. "In this hall there is no room for a man who can't hold his own in some kind of sport. Now, what games might you be good at, you and your friends?"

Loki stepped forth. "I bet nobody in this hall can eat as fast as I can," he said.

"A noble sport," said Utgardsloki, and he told a smallish giant named Logi, to come and try his skill at eating against Loki.

A huge wooden trough piled with meat was brought in. Loki sat down at one side of it, Logi at the other. So fast did the meat disappear into their mouths it looked as if it were being consumed by fire, and it wasn't long before their faces met, right in the middle. But Logi had eaten not only the meat, but the bones and the trough as well, so it was clear who had won the contest.

Utgardsloki shook his head in mock surprise, turned to Tjalfi, and asked what kind of sport he was good at.

"I can outrun any man in this hall," said Tjalfi.

"A noble sport," said Utgardsloki, and he called for a fellow named Hugi and told him to race against Tjalfi.

They all went out into the courtyard to watch the race. Tjalfi ran so fast one could barely see his legs; still he hadn't even run halfway when Hugi reached the goal.

"You ran fast, but not fast enough," said Utgardsloki. "And now," he said, turning to Thor, "we are all eager to see what you can do, for we have heard great tales about you."

"I will drink with you," said Thor. He was thirsty and angry, and he was sure that not even Utgardsloki could swallow as much as he.

"Very well," said Utgardsloki, "but I warn you that my drinking

horn is big. My tall men empty it in one swallow, the medium fellows in two, and there isn't one among the little ones down the hall who cannot empty it in three. Let's see how well you can do, Thor."

An enormous horn was put before Thor. It wasn't so wide, but it was uncommonly long. He lifted it and took one long deep draught. When he could hold his breath no longer, he lifted his head out of the horn and saw to his surprise that it was almost as full as before.

Utgardsloki laughed. "Well drunk," he said, "but had someone told me that Thor wasn't good for a bigger draught, I would not have believed him. Drink again; I know you will empty it this time."

Without saying a word Thor put the horn to his mouth and swallowed and drank until he could hold no more. Again he looked into the horn and saw that the mead had sunk a little, but that was all.

"Well, well," said Utgardsloki, "you did not put on too good a show. Perhaps you are better at something else? Maybe you would like to try to lift my cat off the floor? It is a good sport for little urchins."

A gray cat rose lazily from the floor and stretched itself. With a grim scowl Thor put a hand under its belly and started to lift. The cat was bigger than he had thought. It arched its back higher and higher as Thor lifted. When he had stretched up his hand as far as he could, the cat still had only one paw off the floor.

"Just as I thought," said Utgardsloki. "Our cat is too heavy for Thor."

"You call me an urchin," Thor shouted, and now he was really angry. "Let someone step forth and wrestle with me."

"I don't see a man here who would find it worth while to wrestle with you," said Utgardsloki, looking up and down the hall, "but let old Granny Elle come in. She has thrown bigger fellows than you."

A crooked old crone hobbled into the hall, tackled Thor, and began to wrestle. The harder Thor squeezed her, the firmer she stood her ground. Then she started to use tricks of her own, throwing him this way and that, and it wasn't long before he was down on one knee. The jotuns roared with laughter, and Utgardsloki shouted, "Enough, Thor, don't bother to show us any more of your deeds. Sit down with us anyway and and be our guest."

There was no lack of food and drink, and since Thor was very hungry, he ate a huge meal in spite of the dishonor he had suffered.

He and his companions spent the night in the hall of the jotun, and when morning came, Utgardsloki walked them to the gate.

"Well, Thor, what do you think of your visit to Utgard?" he asked when they were well outside.

"I know you think very little of me, and that is hard to take. All I have earned here is shame," said Thor.

"Now that you are outside," said Utgardsloki, "I will tell you that you did better than you thought. When I heard you were coming, I went out to look you over, and Skrymir, the giant you met in the woods, was no one but me. You thought you hit my head with your hammer, but I confused you and pushed a mountain between me and you. The three deep clefts in that faraway mountain are where the hammer came down. You could not untie my food bag, for I had tied it with a troll knot. Not even your clever Loki saw that Logi, against whom he was eating, was really Wild-fire in person. Tjalfi ran fast, but Hugi was nothing but a thought I sent forth, and who can catch up with a thought? When you tried to empty the horn you never saw that its tip reached down into the sea, and in truth you drank so mightily that the ocean itself ebbed away. So hoodwinked have you been you did not see that the cat was the Midgard's Serpent. You had us all in a fright and the mountains of Midgard were trembling when you stretched yourself so high that the serpent's head and tail barely touched the ground. And a great wonder was it to see you standing up against Elle, for she is Old Age herself. Never will there be a man whom she doesn't throw, if he lives long enough.

"This time I have fooled you, but I hope I'll never meet you again."

In a rage, Thor lifted his hammer, but before he could bring it down Utgardsloki had vanished, and so had his stronghold. Thor and his companions stood alone among mounds and boulders.

Thor was furious and hardly said a word as they trudged the long way back to fetch the billy goats. But Loki wore a malicious smile, looking forward to spreading the news of Thor's unfortunate venture in the land of Utgardsloki. It did not matter to him that he had also been fooled; Thor's shame was worth it.

Thor and the Jotun Rungnir

ONE DAY as Odin was racing Sleipnir, his eight-legged steed, through the air, the jotun Rungnir saw him. He too had a very swift horse that could run through the air. It was a beautiful horse with a golden mane, and Rungnir was very proud of it.

"I bet my horse is faster than yours," he called up to Odin. Odin did not even bother to answer, and that made Rungnir so angry that he jumped upon his horse and sped after Odin to show him. They raced through the air like storm clouds, with Odin ahead but Rungnir close behind. The jotun was so busy spurring his horse that he didn't see that Asgard was straight ahead, and before he knew it, he had stormed through the gate. He stopped short in the courtyard of Asgard, and that was not a safe place for a jotun to be.

Fortunately for Rungnir, Thor was not at home, and Odin, who always observed the laws of hospitality, could not turn a distant traveler away. So he asked Rungnir to come in and refresh himself with some mead. The Aesir offered him Thor's huge drinking horn filled with sweet mead and politely tried to make him feel at ease. To begin with, the jotun minded his manners well, but he had barely emptied the drinking horn before he yelled for Freya to come and fill it again. Then he started to brawl and boast. He would pick up Valhalla and take it with him to Jotunheim, he bellowed, and then he would throw Asgard into the sea, so that all the Aesir would drown. He would spare only Freya and Sif, because he wanted them for wives.

That was too much to take from a jotun, and the Aesir called for Thor. At once he was standing in the doorway, twirling his hammer. The mere sight of him made Rungnir sober.

"I was a fool to enter Asgard without my club," he shouted as he leapt to his feet. "But your father himself invited me in, and it would be dishonorable, Thor, for you to kill an unarmed guest. Meet me tomorrow, and we can fight it out then. I will be waiting for you under the glacier next to my land if you dare to meet me there."

"Get out of Asgard, and be quick about it," Thor growled. "I will deal with you tomorrow."

Rungnir rode home and called his neighbors together. After bragging loudly about having terrified the Aesir, he said that in the morning he would meet Thor in combat, and that he needed a second.

The jotuns put their heads together. If they could only get rid of Thor, they might overrun Asgard. Nobody felt strong enough to be Rungnir's second, however, so they decided to build a monstrous giant out of clay and set him up behind Rungnir as his helper. They worked the whole night, and when at last the clay man was finished, they brought him to life by putting the heart of a mare in his chest. No other creature's heart was big enough to keep the giant alive.

Before dawn Rungnir took his place at the foot of the glacier, with the clay giant looming behind him. At sunrise, Thor and Tjalfi, his servant, arrived. Tjalfi, fastest of all runners, ran ahead of Thor and shouted, "Rungnir, don't hold your shield up high or Thor might strike you from beneath."

When Rungnir heard that, he threw his shield to the ground and stood on it, clutching his club of whetstone in both hands. As Thor approached with a rumble and roar, the jotun bravely stood his ground. But the clay giant trembled and rivers of cold sweat ran down his sides, for although the mare's heart in his chest was big, it held no courage.

Thor hurled his hammer just as Rungnir lifted both his arms and threw the whetstone. The two weapons met in mid-air with an earsplitting crash. Splinters of whetstone flew to all sides, and from them have come all the whetstone mountains in the world. But one splinter went into Thor's head, and he fell to the ground.

His hammer kept flying through the air, hit Rungnir's flint head, and smashed it to bits. As the jotun crashed to the ground, one of his feet fell across Thor's neck. No matter how Thor struggled, he could not get free. There he lay, pinned under the fallen Rungnir.

Tjalfi, meanwhile, easily brought down the frightened clay giant. He simply dug under one of his legs, and the giant fell on his face. All that was left of him were clumps of boulders and clay. Tjalfi then ran to the aid of Thor, but he could not pull him free. So he raced back to Asgard for help.

But when Odin and the other Aesir came, none of them was able to lift the jotun's foot from Thor's neck. Just then Thor's little son Magni, who could not run very fast because his legs were so short, arrived. He was only three years old, but he was already amazingly strong and he lifted Rungnir's foot with one hand. Thor was so proud of his son he gave him Rungnir's golden-maned horse.

When Thor came back to Asgard, he tried in vain to have the splinter of whetstone removed from his head. But there it was stuck and would not move. From then on, whenever somebody carelessly threw a whetstone across the floor, the splinter moved, and Thor, the thunder-god, had a splitting headache. Then thunder roared and lightning flashed, for Thor, like most men, was not one for suffering in silence.

Thor and the Jotun Aegir

ÆGIR, a fierce old jotun, was the lord of the stormy sea; he lived far out in the ocean with his wife and nine daughters. His hall was surrounded by a fence of white sea foam, and its roof was hidden by clouds of screaming sea birds. Rân, his wife, was an evil ogress who wrecked ships and lured sailors to the bottom of the sea. Then she greedily gathered their gold from the ocean floor and heaped it up on her hearth, where it gleamed brighter than fire.

Aegir's nine daughters were wild but graceful maidens who loved the roaring gales. Gaily they leapt into the breakers and rode the waves that raged against the shores. Their red hair glittered lovely and warm in the sun, but they were pitiless and cold, and laughingly overturned ships so that their mother could have more gold.

Aegir was on friendly terms with the Aesir, since they had kept him in power, and indeed they counted the jotun as one of them. He was a welcome guest at Asgard, but he never invited the Aesir to his hall. At last the Aesir decided it was time Aegir gave a feast for them. Thor brought him the message, and he was not altogether polite.

"You had better get busy brewing and baking," he said. And he looked at the jotun with such a scowl that Aegir was afraid to say "no." Trying to think up a good excuse, he squirmed and squinted, and, since his eyes were small and ugly, that did not make them any prettier.

At last he said, "I don't have a caldron big enough to brew beer for so many highly honored guests, but if you can bring me one I shall be glad to feast all of you." For he knew that no one but Hymir, one of the wildest of the jotuns, had such a caldron, and that he would never willingly lend it to one of the Aesir. But Thor said he would bring a caldron and returned to Asgard.

Now Tyr, Thor's half brother, was a grandson of Hymir, and he remembered that there were huge caldrons hanging in Hymir's hall. "I will go with you," he said to Thor, "and if I choose my words well, my grandfather might let you have one."

So Thor and Tyr set off for Jotunheim together and came to Hymir's hall. His wife, a dreadful hag with nine hundred heads, stood blocking the door. But her daughter, who was beautiful and gentle, came forward

to let them in. She was Tyr's mother, and when she had greeted him fondly, she asked what errand had brought him and Thor to faraway Jotunheim. When they told her why they had come, she shook her head but said she would try to help them.

"Hurry and hide behind a pillar," she said. "The old one will soon be home, and he does not care for strangers in his hall."

Thor hated to hide from a jotun, but he and Tyr did as they were told. They had hardly gotten out of sight when Hymir stormed through the door. Icicles cracked and tinkled in the frozen forest on his chin, and his mood was just as icy as his beard.

"Come, Father, sit by the fire and warm yourself," said Tyr's mother. "I have good news for you. Your grandson Tyr has come to see us, and he has brought his kinsman, Thor, with him. They are behind that pillar, waiting to greet you."

As soon as Hymir heard Thor's name he sprang to his feet and stared down the hall. So fierce was his stare that it split the pillar, and eight huge caldrons that had been hanging from the crossbeam crashed to the floor. All but the very biggest of them broke into pieces.

Then Thor and Tyr stepped forward and greeted him politely. Hymir grunted and snarled, but he kept his manners. Even a jotun had to abide by the laws of hospitality, and he had three whole oxen put on the spit. Thor ate two of them all by himself and washed them down with barrels of beer and mead.

"It seems to me that you have eaten a man-sized meal," Hymir said to Thor. "Now if we want to eat tomorrow, you and I had better go fishing for whales." Thor had nothing against that, and the next morning the two of them set off. They didn't use minnows for bait; Thor had nothing less than the head of a steer tied onto his hook! Each of them grasped a pair of oars and they rowed straight into the wild and open sea. When at last all land had disappeared from sight, they pulled in their oars and threw out their lines.

Hymir soon had two fat whales wriggling on his hook, and he heaved them into the boat. But Thor's hook, baited with the steer head, sank all the way to the bottom. Suddenly the sea all around them started boiling, and there was such a jerk on Thor's line that his hand slammed against the gunwhale. Angrily he pulled with all his enormous strength, and what did he pull up but the mighty Midgard's Serpent itself! Thor

and the serpent glared at each other with red, glowing eyes; then Thor swung his hammer and threw it at the monster's skull. The serpent let out a howl so loud that earth and sea trembled, and the mountains rang, far in the distance. Hymir, his teeth chattering with fear, cut the fishing line before Thor could strike another blow, and in a foaming whirlpool the serpent sank back to the bottom of the sea.

Thor glowered darkly but did not say a word. In silence they rowed to shore. When they landed, Hymir said, "Now let us share the work." Thor did not even answer. He grabbed the boat with whales, oars, dipper, and bilge water, and pulled it far up on the shore. Then he threw the whales over his shoulders, stuck the oars under his arms, and tramped off to Hymir's hall. Hymir could hardly keep up with Thor, even with his hands empty. The hag with the many heads boiled the whales, and there was enough food to go around for that dinner!

When Hymir had eaten his fill and had wiped the whale oil out of his beard, Tyr asked him to lend them a caldron. "The feats of mighty Thor have earned that favor," he added.

"It doesn't take great strength to row a bit and carry a couple of whales a short little way," said Hymir sourly. Then he scowled at Thor.

"But if you can break my crystal goblet, you really are as strong as they claim," he said. "If you can do that I will give you a caldron."

Thor took the goblet and threw it against one of the pillars in the hall. It shot through the pillar and fell to the floor, and there wasn't even a nick in it.

"Throw it at Hymir's head," Tyr's mother whispered into his ear. "Nothing in the world is as hard as his head."

Thor swung the goblet and threw it with all his might, and when the goblet hit Hymir's head it broke into a thousand rock-crystal splinters.

Hymir groaned loudly. Not only had he lost his precious goblet, he had lost his only remaining caldron as well. But he had no way of stopping Thor from swinging the caldron over his head and walking out of the hall with Tyr following. The caldron was so heavy that Thor's feet sank deep into the ground, and it was so big that the handles clanked against his heels. Even Thor had trouble carrying it.

They had not walked far when they heard a noise behind them. Looking back, they saw a swarm of jotuns and many-headed trolls running after them. Even more of them leapt up from clefts in the ground and from behind boulders, and Hymir led them all. Thor set down the

caldron and swung his hammer. Every time he threw the hammer, it knocked down a jotun or a troll, and in no time at all he had made an end of Hymir and all his followers. Then he swung the caldron over his head again and carried it straight to Aegir's hall.

Aegir kept his word; he did not dare do otherwise. He brewed beer and mead and prepared a feast so splendid that the Aesir had never seen its equal. The shimmering gold on the hearth lit up the hall. The drinking horns rolled up and down the tables from hand to hand and filled themselves when they were empty. And like will-o'-the-wisps Aegir's two servants were everywhere at once, heaping food before the guests. It was the best feast ever, and Aegir, in a high good mood, promised the Aesir he would prepare them such a feast every year.

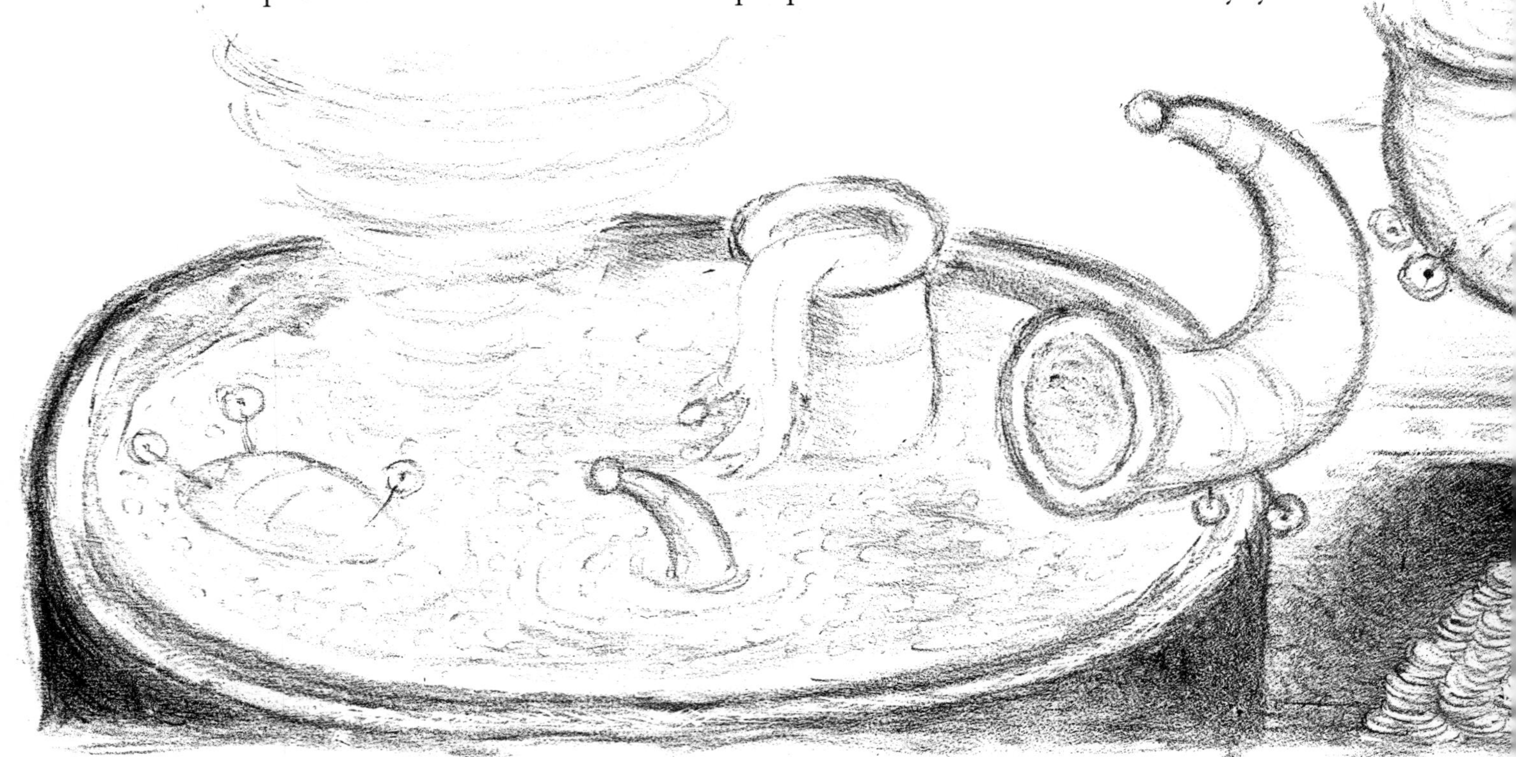

The Death of Balder

LIFE AT ASGARD became ever busier as time went on; neither gods nor goddesses now had time to sit on the greensward of Ida and play with golden chessmen. They had their hands full guiding the ever-increasing number of people on earth. There were more and more battlefields for Odin and his Valkyries to watch over, and Thor was always away killing jotuns and trolls. Loki was going from bad to worse, getting ever more malicious. And while he had always loved attention, now he flew into a frenzy of rage if he wasn't praised for his clever ideas. Only gentle Balder did not change.

But then Balder began to be haunted by bad dreams. This worried the other Aesir greatly, for they feared that the dreams foreboded evil for him. And they could not take steps to protect him unless they knew what the dreams meant. They met in council at Yggdrasil's foot, and there it was decided that Odin himself must go to the grave of a volva, a wise woman who had long been dead. He must bring her back by his magic and force her to reveal what Balder's dreams meant.

In the blackness of night Odin rode to the burial mound of the volva. He sang a magic chant and her ghost rose moaning and groaning from the hollow ground. Wearily she spoke: "Balder's days are numbered. Hel has already prepared a seat for him in her dark world." And she sank back into her grave.

With a sad heart Odin rode home to Asgard and told the Aesir there was nothing they could do; Balder would soon be leaving for Hel. But Frigg, Balder's mother, refused to give up hope. She went out into the world and made all things, living and lifeless, promise not to harm her son. Water, fire, stones, and metals, diseases, plants, and trees, and all the animals gave her their pledges. Joyfully Frigg returned to Asgard, and the Aesir were happy again. Now nothing evil could happen to their beloved Balder.

The Aesir were so sure of it that they playfully formed a ring around Balder and pelted him with pebbles, rocks, spears, and axes—they even shot arrows at him! All fell harmlessly at his feet, and Balder stood smiling as if he had been showered with flowers. It was a marvelous game and the Aesir laughed and enjoyed themselves. But not Loki. Jealousy gnawed at his evil heart. He sneaked away, disguised himself as an old crone, hobbled up to Frigg, and said, "How wonderfully well you have protected your son. But are you sure that *everything* in the world has promised not to harm him?"

"I am quite sure," Frigg replied. "Everything except the little mistletoe. It is so small and soft that I didn't bother to take it in oath."

"Aha, this will be Balder's undoing," Loki thought as he hobbled away in a hurry. He quickly found a mistletoe plant and made a sharp arrow from one of its twigs. Then he returned to the Aesir, who were

still at play around Balder.

Hod, Balder's blind brother, stood aside by himself. "Why don't you take part in the game?" Loki asked him.

"How can I?" answered Hod. "I cannot see where Balder stands. Besides I have no weapon."

"Here," said Loki, "take my bow and arrow and I shall guide your aim." With Loki's help, Hod pulled the bowstring and listened for the soft sound of the arrow falling to the ground. Instead he heard a dull thud and a cry of anguish from all the Aesir. Never had an arrow found its mark so well; the little twig had pierced Balder's heart.

In horror the Aesir turned and stared at Hod, who was again standing by himself, for Loki had hurried away. Their arms fell limply to their sides and they wept. How could their world survivè without gentle Balder.

At last the Aesir pulled themselves together and began to prepare a stately funeral for Balder aboard his great ship. With their heads bowed low they carried him down to the shore where the ship lay beached. All the gods and goddesses, all the elves and dwarfs, even some trolls and jotuns, came to bid Balder a last farewell. Only Loki was nowhere to be seen.

They built a pyre under the mast and covered it with Balder's treasures. But when they tried to launch the ship, it stood as if it were nailed to the ground. No one could budge it, not even Thor. They had to send to Jotunheim for the ogress Hyrrokkin.

She came at once, riding on a wild wolf with a serpent for a bridle, and she gave the ship such a hard shove that sparks flew from the rollers and all the land trembled. Once the ship was afloat, Balder's body was placed on the pyre. When Nanna, his wife, saw this, her heart broke and she died; she could not live without him. So the Aesir sadly laid her down at her husband's side.

Then Odin took off his golden armlet, put it on Balder's chest as a parting gift, and lit the pyre. Thor swung his hammer three times over the fire and blessed it. The ropes were cut and the flaming ship drifted out to sea with Odin's black ravens fluttering about the mast. Aegir's daughters tossed high their white scarves of sea foam, and everyone wept for Balder as the ship sank down to Hel.

Odin's sorrow was great, but Frigg's was greater still, for she blamed herself. Why had she neglected the weak little mistletoe? And was there no way to undo her carelessness?

"Who wants to win my everlasting love?" she asked the sons of Odin. "Who dares to travel the dark road to Hel and beg her to let Balder return?"

Odin's son Hermod, who had great courage, stepped forward and said that he would travel the road to Hel. So they saddled Odin's horse Sleipnir for him and he galloped away. For nine days and nights he rode across dismal swamps and through haunted valleys. On the ninth night he came to a bridge paved with gold which spanned an icy river coming from Niflheim. It was a bridge that only dead men on their way to Hel must cross. Without fear, Hermod started across it, but its guardian, a giantess sitting on the other bank, challenged him.

"Who makes my bridge ring so loudly?" she cried. "A hundred dead horsemen make less din than your steed. You are not a dead man;

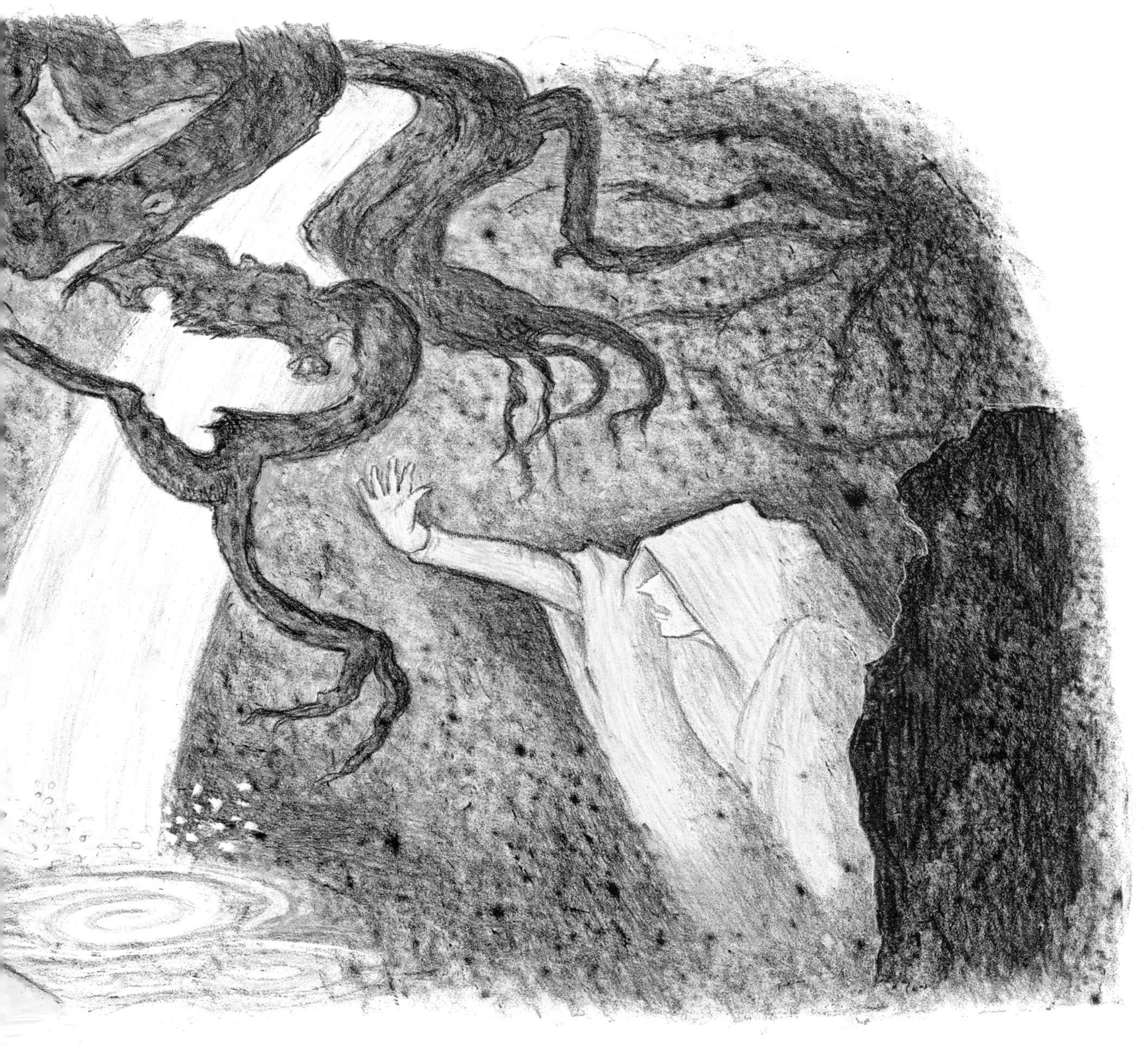

the color in your cheeks gives you away!" She rose to stop him.

"I am Hermod, son of Odin. I am on my way to Hel to seek my brother Balder," he shouted back.

"Pass, then," said the giantess. "I saw your fair brother crossing the bridge. The way to Hel is down and north," she added, pointing the way, for even she was grieving for Balder.

Hermod followed the road which soon led him to the gate of Hel's realm. There the fearful dog Garm stood snarling and straining at his leash, but Hermod spurred his horse and Sleipnir leapt high over the gate. At the doorstep he dismounted and walked into the hall of Hel.

Stony-faced and dreadful to behold, Hel sat on her throne. Across from her sat Balder, with Nanna at his side. She had a wreath of wilted flowers on her head, and a horn of sweet mead stood before them, untouched. They sat without stirring, as if in a dream.

Hermod greeted Hel and began to speak. For a whole night he pleaded with her to let Balder go. He told her how much the Aesir grieved over their loss and how all nature was weeping for him. At last she rose from her throne, and the gold that entwined her huge body flared like flames as she spoke. "If it be true that Balder is so beloved that all things, living and lifeless, weep for him, I will let him return to the living. But if there is one thing that will not weep, then he must remain with me," she said.

Hermod prepared to leave, and Balder rose and led him through the door. He thanked Hermod for coming such a long way. Then he gave him Draupnir, the golden armlet, and asked him to take it back to Odin, because only the living have need of gold.

Hermod rode back to Asgard as fast as Sleipnir could carry him and Hel's words brought new hope to the Aesir. They had no doubt that all things in the world would join them in weeping for Balder, and Frigg at once sent messengers to tell all things to weep Balder out of Hel.

Every creature and every thing wept—men and women, beasts, birds, trees, flowers, stones, metals—everything living and lifeless shed tears for Balder.

But as the messengers were returning to Asgard, they came upon an old crone sitting all alone in a cave. When asked to weep, she refused to shed a single tear, but rasped, "Never has Balder done anything for me. Let Hel keep what she has." She called herself Thokk, but she was really Loki in disguise.

And so Balder had to remain in the dark realm of Hel. There he was soon joined by Hod, for, after the rules of the Aesir, life must be paid with life. Vali, Odin's youngest son, avenged Balder's death and sent Hod to Hel.

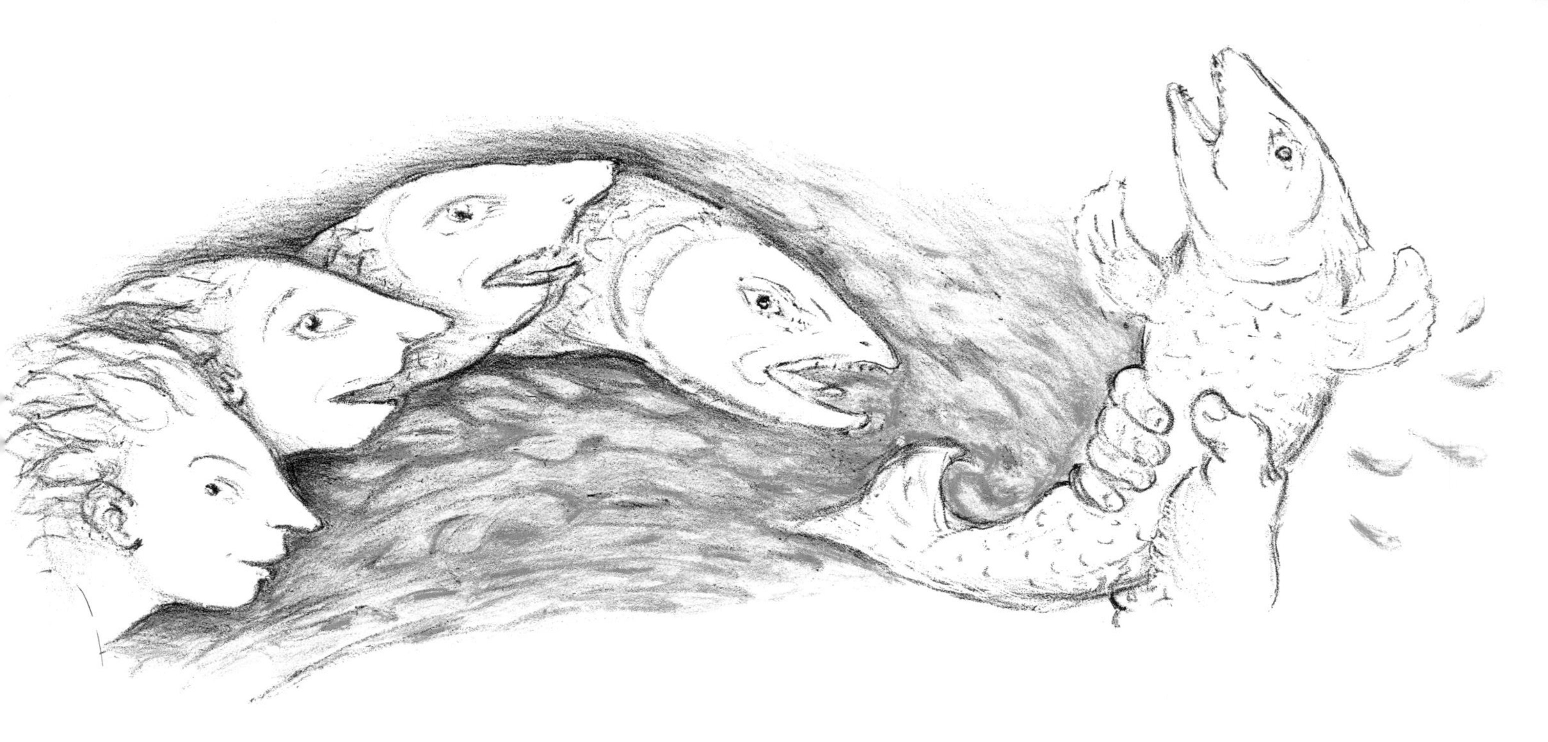

Loki's Punishment

LIFE DID, after all, go on without Balder. Time passed and once again it was the day of Aegir's feast. All the gods and goddesses went to his hall, and many of the elves. Only Thor was missing; he was off fighting jotuns and trolls.

Aegir had outdone himself preparing the feast. More gold than ever blazed on the hearth, the drinking horns rolled up and down the table, and Aegir's two servants plied every guest with more food than he could eat. Everyone was having a good time; they had nothing but nice words for each other and high praise for the host and for his servants. Loki was again filled with jealousy. No one was saying kind things to him or listening to his witty words. At last in a wild fury he jumped on one of the servants and killed him.

Angrily the Aesir rose. They could not harm him, since Odin's presence made the hall a sacred place. Besides he was Odin's blood brother. But they chased him out. In a huff, Loki slunk around outside the hall, listening to the talk inside. The gods were again praising each other, but not one nice word did he hear about himself. Full of spite, he went back inside, walked straight up to Odin, and asked to be served.

"Dear brother Odin," he sneered, "have you forgotten that at the beginning of time we vowed never to accept a favor not also offered to the other? Now, who is offering *me* a horn filled with beer?"

His head bent low, Odin told one of his sons to offer a horn to Loki. Loki emptied it, and that made him bolder still. He heaped abuse on the

Aesir and did not spare the goddesses, either, and when Odin tried to silence him, he turned on him.

"Odin," he shouted, "you are neither as great nor as wise as you try to make us believe. Many a time I have seen you give victory to the lesser man because he flattered you."

"Loki, be silent," said Odin. "I have seen you playing the part of females. Who but Loki is the mother of my horse Sleipnir?"

There was no insult greater than saying that a man had played the part of a female. Loki turned pale but quickly paid Odin back. "And I remember when you flew about in the company of witches and practiced black magic," he shouted.

"Keep quiet, you two," said Frigg. "These things belong to the past and should be left alone."

At that Loki turned on Frigg and spat out, "I shall tell you more about the past. Had it not been for me your dear son Balder would have been here with you today. It was I who found out about the mistletoe, I gave Hod his arrow and aimed it, and who do you think was the crone who refused to weep him out of Hel?" Then he turned on the others and screamed at each in turn, not omitting Sif and her husband Thor, who was not there. In his rage he forgot that Thor would appear whenever he was mentioned by name. Immediately there was a rumble and a peal of thunder, and Thor stood in the doorway, hammer in hand. The only thing that Loki feared was Thor's hammer, so he quickly turned to leave, but not before he had taunted Thor, too.

"Mighty Thor," he jeered, "you were not so mighty the night you slept in the jotun's mitt," then he slipped out before Thor could throw his hammer. "Aegir" he called back over his shoulder, "never again shall you feast the Aesir; fire shall devour all that you own." And he ran off into the faraway mountains to hide.

"Now the cup is full," the Aesir cried. "Loki must be punished."

To find his hiding place, Odin mounted his High Seat, the Lidskjalf, and looked over the world. Far in the distance, beside a waterfall, a strange little house with an open door on every side caught his eye. He looked closely, and saw Loki sitting inside by a fire, tying strings into loops and knots.

The Aesir stormed off to catch him, but Loki was keeping watch through the four open doors and saw them coming. He threw what he was making into the fire, jumped into the waterfall, and changed himself into a salmon. "They will never catch me on their hook," he sniggered. Loki did not worry about being caught in a net because no one had ever made one as yet. Indeed that was the thing he had been inventing, and he had just burned it.

But this time Loki was caught by his own cleverness. For when the Aesir saw the traces of the net in the ashes they understood that this was a device for catching fish and made one for themselves. They threw it into the waterfall and dragged it downstream. But Loki, the salmon, slid in among the boulders at the bottom of the river and laughed as the net passed over him.

"We'll catch him yet," said the Aesir. "Let us put some bark on top of the net to make it float, and stones to weigh down its bottom. Then we will drag it down to the sea while Thor wades behind it."

In this way Loki was chased all the way down to the open sea. There whales and sharks and sea monsters lay watching for fish to catch and devour, so Loki turned to swim upstream again. He made a desperate leap over the top of the net, but Thor's hand shot out and caught him by his slippery tail.

Now the Aesir showed no mercy. They squeezed Loki back into his true shape and took him to a dark and dismal cave. They placed him across three sharp ledges, bound him securely, and hung a poisonous serpent over his head so that its venom dripped down on his face. There they left Loki to lie and suffer.

Sigunn, his loyal wife, stood by him and tried to ease his pain. She would catch the venom in a cup, but when the cup was full, she had to empty it. Then the poison dripping on Loki's face made him squirm and tear so hard at his fetters that the whole world trembled. Men on Midgard would pray to be saved from the earthquake, but on Asgard the Aesir would think of Balder and turn away with grim faces.

Ragnarokk, the Destiny of the Gods

YGGDRASIL, the world tree, trembled and its evergreen leaves began to wilt. Odin was deeply worried. Once again he, the father of gods and men, had broken his sacred word. He had allowed the Aesir to lay hands on Loki; for even though Loki was evil, he was his foster brother, and they had sworn eternal kinship. The world of the Aesir was built on honor, and with honor gone, the Aesir were no longer high and holy. Their world was falling apart.

In deep gloom Odin went to the grave of the wise woman, the volva, and to the head of Mimir, and asked for advice. But all he could hear was: "Ax time, sword time, ere the world fall; wind time, wolf time! Do you know more now or not?"

Then Odin knew that Ragnarokk, the day of reckoning when the destiny of the gods would be decided, was fast approaching. Soon the Aesir must face the forces of destruction and win over them, or be themselves destroyed.

There was no more kindness among gods or men since gentle Balder had passed over to the gloomy realm of Hel. Brother could no longer trust brother. In their lust for gold men stole from each other and killed each other, and bloody wars raged all over the earth. Odin and his Valkyries rushed from battlefield to battlefield to gather as many heroes as they could to fight in the last battle. Even the vast hall of Valhalla was getting crowded.

Thor was as busy as his father, forever on the go, fighting jotuns and trolls. For the monsters were getting bolder, drawing ever closer, pelting the world with snow and ice. Their frosty breath spread an icy fog over the earth, shutting out the warm rays of the sun.

And a winter came that lasted for three years. Deep snow covered the ground; nothing could sprout, nothing could grow. Men no longer fought for gold, but for food, and Hel's hall was filled to bursting with all those who had died of starvation.

Then, early one morning, long before daybreak, the golden cock of Asgard stretched out his neck and crowed loudly. An answer came echo-

ing up through the ground from the soot-black cock that perched on the roof of Hel's hall. The day of Ragnarokk had come.

The earth split open, all the way to the world of the dead, and all the bonds of the world broke with a twang. Garm, the hound of Hel, leapt free from his leash, Fenris the wolf shook off his magic fetter, and Loki rose free from his ledge. No longer was anyone bound by anything.

In deepest Niflheim, the dragon Nidhogg gnawed and gnawed at the root of the world tree. Yggdrasil trembled and groaned and lost all its leaves. "Woe," cried the Norns at the foot of the tree. They covered their faces and stopped spinning the threads of life.

From his watch on top of the rainbow Heimdall now saw enemies coming from all directions. He lifted high his horn and blew with all his might. The blasts of the Gjallarhorn shrilled through all worlds, and the Aesir leapt to their feet and donned their battle gear. Valhalla's many doors sprang open and out rushed Odin's vast army of heroes. With loud battle cries they fell into formation behind Odin.

The huge army of gods and heroes marched through the gates of Asgard. First came Odin on his eight-legged steed, his single eye gleaming like the sun. At his side strode Thor with enormous steps. He swung his hammer and gnashed his teeth as his eyes fell on the welter of jotuns and many-headed trolls rolling down from the east.

From the frothing sea the Midgard's Serpent slithered up on land. There he was met by his brother Fenris. By now the wolf was so enormous that his gaping jaws touched the earth and the vault of the sky; and had there been room his jaws would have gaped wider still. Side by side the two dreadful monsters pushed forward.

Out of the north came a ghoulish ship, the Nagelfar. Its sides were covered with clippings of finger- and toenails, and it was manned by a crew of ghosts. Standing at the rudder and sailing the ship straight through the raging sea was Loki, coming back for revenge.

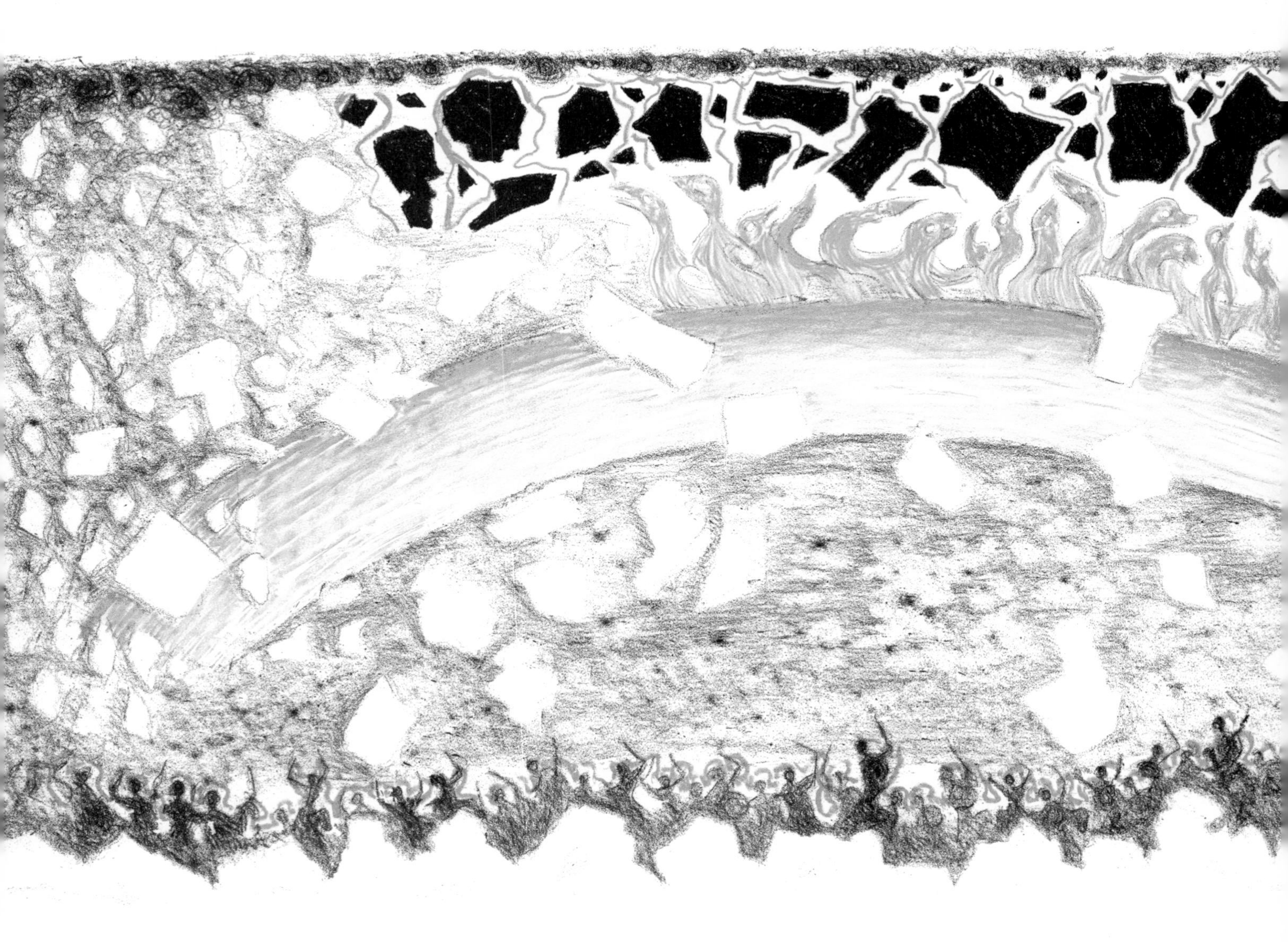

The din of the monsters was so loud that the vault of the sky split open. Through the crack burst Surt, ruler of Muspelheim, the world of fire. He swung his flaming sword, and it set fire to everything it touched as he rushed toward the rainbow bridge. Behind him surged his warriors, horde upon horde of fire demons, all set upon conquering Asgard. But when they stormed the shimmering bridge it broke and fell.

Surt and his warriors then made for the wide field of Vigrid, the greatest field in the world. One hundred miles long and one hundred miles wide, it was a proper battlefield for gods and giants. There the fire demons were joined by the hordes of trolls and jotuns, ghosts and monsters. In row upon row, they waited for the Aesir to come and give battle.

Led by Odin, the huge army of gods and heroes thundered up the field. Odin made straight for the gaping jaws of Fenris. But before he could throw his spear down the wolf's horrible gullet, the monster lurched

forward and swallowed him.

Thor could not come to his father's aid; he had his hands full fighting the Midgard's Serpent. Time and again he threw his hammer at the hissing head, until at last the serpent gave up its breath and died. Thor lived only long enough to stagger nine steps backward. Then he fell to the ground, killed by the serpent's poisonous breath.

Odin's son Vidar avenged his father. He had an enormous boot made from the remnants of shoe leather that good men on earth had saved. When he leapt forward and thrust his foot into the mouth of the wolf, he tore the powerful jaws apart and split the monster's head.

The archenemies, Loki and Heimdall, fell, pierced by each other's weapons. Tyr and Garm, the hound of Hel, also killed each other.

Frey fell an easy prey when the demon Surt thrust his flaming sword through him. Frey's only weapon was a pair of antlers, for he had given away his golden sword to win the love of Gerd.

Odin's vast army of heroes fought as long as there was a man standing, though jotuns and trolls pelted them with blocks of ice, with boulders, yes, even with mountains.

At last the battle ended. Most of the Aesir and all of Odin's warriors lay dead, and the sound of the goddesses weeping filled the world.

Then the two jotuns in wolf's clothing caught up with sun and moon and swallowed them.

The Aesir world was plunged into darkness, and Yggdrasil, the world tree, broke and fell. Surt lifted his flaming sword and flung fire over everything. The sea rose above the mountains and fell crashing over the land. The air trembled, the stars were ripped from the sky as burning earth disappeared under the waves, and the sacred halls of Asgard toppled and fell.

Out of the depths rose Nidhogg, the dragon of destruction. For a while it hovered over the fallen world, then sank back into the void.

All that was left of the world of the Aesir was the field of Ida, where their glittering halls had stood. There the Aesir who had not been destroyed gathered again.

When the earth split open, Balder, the gentle, came up from Hel, leading his blind brother, Hod. They were joined by Magni and Modi, Thor's young sons, and by Odin's sons Vidar and Vali, youngest of the Aesir. And Hoenir, Odin's brother, came back from the faraway world of the Vanir to stand by his kinsmen.

Quietly, the last of the Aesir walked over the field of Ida, looking at the ruins of their once glittering halls and talking about the great deeds of their fathers. There, on the greensward, they found the golden chessmen with which they had played in the old days of power and glory. Now they had no one to lead, no one to guard; they had nothing to do but play chess and think back. So they sat down in the gray twilight and played peaceful games with their golden chessmen.

A New World

AND IT happened that a new day dawned.

Before she was swallowed by the jotun in wolf's clothing, sun had rapidly given birth to a daughter. The little daughter grew as big and bright as her mother had been, and she rose shining in the sky. A new moon and new stars appeared, and a new rainbow bridged the desolate sea and the high heavens far above the field of Ida.

And slowly a new earth rose from the sea.

It was a green and lovely new earth, where seeds sprouted in unsown fields and eagles soared high over crystal-clear brooks. Again animals roamed through the forests and fields, and fish gamboled in the sea.

Then out of the secret grove of Hodmimir stepped a maiden and a youth. They were Lif and Lifthrasir—"Life" and the "Stubborn Will to Live." They alone among mankind had escaped the destruction of Ragnarokk. They had hidden under the bark of trees and had found their food in the morning dew. Their descendants would people the new earth.

Lif and Lifthrasir did not lift their heads and hands in prayer to the Aesir gods. They prayed to God Almighty, who had stepped out from above to rule all the worlds in eternity. He would gather around him all good souls to live in glory forever at Gimlé, the paradise that gleamed like a jewel in the sky, far above anything else.

The harsh and warlike days of the Aesir world were gone. But for hundreds of years, memories of the Aesir gods and of their foes lived on in the north. People were certain that behind the closed doors of the mountains, jotuns and trolls were hiding. And men, lifting their heads on a stormy night to look at the raging clouds, might glimpse instead a phantom band of wild horsemen, led by "one" on an eight-legged steed.

Reader's Companion

After most entries, the phonetic pronunciation of the Norse word is given in parenthesis, followed in italics by the literal, ancient meaning of the word.

Aegir (*ai*-geer) *sea* An ancient jotun, he was lord of the stormy seas. His wife was Rân, and his nine daughters, who had poetic names such as "the one who glitters" and "the one whose hair is red in the evening sun," personified the waves. Aesir, 120; feast for, 126, 137; daughters, 132; family, 120; Thor, 120, 126

Aesir (*ai*-seer) *spirits* The Norse gods whose cult was brought to the north by an Indo-European tribe from the east. The emphasis of the cult was definitely masculine, and the virtues it exalted had to do with preserving the honor of one's name, avenging the death of any kinsman, and waging war with ferocious courage. The long hair of the Aesir gods was considered a sign of manly power. 10-11; Aegir's feast, 126, 137; councils, 34-35; first, 18, 27 *see* Hoenir, Lodur *and* Odin; hatred of, 20; home, 27 *see* Asgard; honor, 54, 71, 140; judge, 54; Loki, 42, punishment of, 138-39; mankind, relationship, 30; mortality, 30; offspring, 21, 24-25; population, 33; Ragnarokk, 144, 146, 150; relatives *see* Vanir; rules, 136; ship *see* Skidbladnir, 46; Thor, 40; Vanir: conflict, 58-59, relationship, 64; wall around, 68-70, 71; wives and daughters *see* Asynjer

Alfheim (*ahlf*-hame) *home of elves* The home of Frey, god of fertility, and of the light-elves, who were also friendly spirits of fertility. 10, 24, 61, 96

Angerboda (*ahng*-er-boh-dah) *bringer of anguish* An ogress, she was Loki's wife in Jotunheim, and mother of the three monsters, Fenris, Hel and the Midgard's Serpent. 42; children, 50

Animals creation, 25

Asgard (*ahs*-gahr) *farm of the Aesir gods* The home of the Aesir gods. In its center was the open field of Ida, around which stood the thirteen halls of the gods. It was protected by a wall and reached by a rainbow bridge. 10, 27, 34, 35, 36-37, 42; fall of, 150; life at, 128; sacred field of Ida, 58

Ask (ahsk) *ash tree* The first man, who was created from an ash tree by the first three Aesir gods. All human beings in the world of the Aesir were descended from him and Embla, the first woman. 27

Asynjer (*oh*-sin-yer) *feminine form of Aesir* The wives and daughters of the Aesir gods. Their long hair was considered precious, and cutting any woman's hair was thought to be one of the worst crimes that could be committed against her. 34-35, 90

Balder (*bahl*-der) *lord* The son of Odin and Frigg, he was the god of light and of peace. His wife was Nanna, their son Forsete. His home in Asgard was called "the far-gleaming." 33, 54; characteristics, 54; death, 131-32, avengement, 136, effect of, 140; dreams, 128; family, 54; in Hel, 132, 134-35, 136, 138, return from, 150; Loki, 138; mother, 128; Skade, 92

Balderblom (*bahl*-der-blom) *flower of Balder* A very beautiful little white flower that grows in the mountains of Scandinavia. 54

Baldness shame of, 44-45

Barre (*bahr*-reh) *barley, grain* The sacred barley patch where Frey and Gerd met in a Norse explanation of the mystery of spring's flowering out of winter's frozen earth. 98

Battles(fields) 72, 73, 128, 140; first, 58; Vigrid, 146

Beauty goddess of *see* Freya

Berserk (*ber*-serk) *bearskin cloak* A man in a raging fury who wore a bearskin cloak, thereby acquiring the strength of a bear. 78

Birds creation, 25

Bragi (*brah*-gee) *song* The son of Odin and the jotun maiden Gunnlod, he was the god of poetry. His wife was Idunn. 30, 66; characteristics, 66; voice, 89, 90

Brokk (brock) *hunchback* A gnome who made a wager with Loki, betting his brother Sindri's skill as a smith against his own head. 46-48, 49

Cats 114, 116

Chessmen golden, 128, 150

Copenhagen 83

Day creation, 21

Death decrees, 30; payment for in gold, 91

Denmark 82

Destiny of the gods *see* Ragnarokk

Draupnir (*drawp*-neer) *dripping* Odin's magic armring that was made by the gnome Sindri. Every ninth night eight new bracelets dropped from the armring. 48, 136

Earth 34; creation, 21; new, 152. *see also* Midgard

Edda (*ed*-dah) *great-grandmother* There are two Eddas, the Poetic Edda and the Prose Edda, which contain the Norse myths. The myths were an oral tradition between the time the Indo-European tribe that brought the cult settled in the north and the eleventh century A.D., when they were first written down in the Poetic Edda. Thus they were recorded at a very late stage, and many of them already reflect a gradual transition from myth to fairy tale. The original meanings were often already blurred or forgotten, and many of the stories had been lost as the once important gods they celebrated had long ago sunk into obscurity. (*see* Ull) Moreover, there is a possibility that some elements did not come from the ancient tradition at all, but were instead contemporary insertions reflecting the Christian church's efforts to stamp out old pagan beliefs. (*See also* Ragnarokk, Gimlé) 11

Eight-legged steed 71 *see* Sleipnir

Eir (air) *mercy, forebearing* The goddess of healing. 80

Elle (*ell*-lee) *old age* Old Age in the form of an old woman with whom Thor wrestled at Utgardsloki's hall. 115, 116

Elves Also referred to as light-elves, these were friendly spirits of fertility. Ghostlike and full of magic, they had cloaks of invisibility and belts that made them irresistibly attractive. 137; characteristics, 24; creation, 24; Frey, 61

Embla (*em*-blah) *alder* The first woman, who was created from an alder tree by the first three Aesir gods. All human beings in the world of the Aesir were descended from her and Ask, the first man. 27

Fays of Destiny *see* Norns

Fenris (*fen*-riss) *from the swamp* A monstrous wolf, offspring of Loki and Angerboda, who was confined to an isolated island by the Aesir. 50, 52, 54, 77, 143, 144, 146-47

Fertility god of, 60

Fish creation, 25

Forests origin, 21

Forsete (*for*-seh-teh) *he who sits in the front seat* The son of Balder and Nanna, he was the chief judge of the Aesir. 54

Frey (fry) *the foremost* The son of the Vanir god Njord, he was the god of fertility. His golden boar plowed the earth and made it green, while Frey sent sunshine and rain to earth. His wife was the jotun maiden Gerd, and his home was Alfheim. 59, 60-61; death, 147; Gerd, 97-98, 147; golden boar, 48; home, 96; marriage, 96-98; sword, 97, 98

Freya (*fry*-ah) *lady, mistress* The daughter of the Vanir god Njord, she was the goddess of beauty and love. Her husband, who had vanished, was Od, and her daughter was Noss. Her home in Asgard was called "field of men." The Norse said that the Milky Way was Freya's necklace. 10, 59, 62-63, 68, 69, 71, 84; beauty, 89, 90; falcon wings, 100; golden tears, 63, 101; hostess, 80; necklace, 84, 86, 100, 101; Rungnir, 117; Thor's hammer, 100-2

Frigg (frig) *lady, mistress* Odin's wife and Balder's mother, she was the highest in rank of the goddesses. She was the goddess of matrimony and looked after homes, and was thought of as always spinning yarn. The stars known as the Belt of Orion were said by the Norse to be Frigg's distaff. 37, 128, 130, 132, 136, 138; goddesses, 80, 82; ladies-in-waiting, 80; Lidskjalf, 96

Frost giants 9-10, 35. *See* Jotuns.

Fulla (*full*-lah) *carrying a goblet* A lady-in-waiting to Frigg, she cared for Frigg's jewels and shoes, and shared Frigg's secrets. 80

Funeral pyre 132

Fyn (fune) A Danish island west of Sjaelland, it was Odin's favorite island. There was a sanctuary to Odin there, at Odense, and Hans Christian Andersen was born there. 82

Garm (gahrm) *barking* The howling hound that guarded the gate to Hel. 50, 135, 143; death, 147

Gefjon (*geff*-yone) *giving* A goddess identified with Frigg, who, with the help of her four sons, plowed the Danish island, Sjaelland, out of the mainland of Sweden and transported it to its present position. 82-83

Geirrod (*gay*-rod) *spear-thrower* A jotun who tried to outwit and overcome Thor by getting him to come to Jotunheim without any weapons. 104-7; daughters, 106, 107; Loki, 104-5; Thor, 107

Gerd (gaird) *fence enclosing tilled land* The daughter of the jotun Gymir, she became the wife of Frey in a Norse explanation of the mystery of spring's flowering out of winter's icy earth. Gerd represents the frozen seed, brought to life by Frey's gentle rains and warm sunshine. 96-98, 147

Ghosts 144

Giants 110-11, 112; clay, 118, 119 *see also* Jotuns, frost giants.

Gimlé (*gim*-le) *roof set with jewels, stars* The uppermost heaven from which one god ruled the new world that appeared after the destruction of Ragnarokk. The concept sits uncomfortably with the major part of Nordic mythology, and there is at the least a possibility that Ragnarokk, the new world, and Gimlé were added to the body of pagan tradition as part of the Christian church's effort to establish itself in Scandinavia. *See also* Ragnarokk, Edda. 10, 152

Ginungagap (*gin*-noon-gah-*gahp*) *gaping chaos* The primeval pit of chaos between Niflheim, the world of ice, and Muspelheim, the world of fire. Out of Ginungagap came the first two living creatures, Ymir and the ice-cow. 12-14, 20

Gjallarhorn (*yal*-lar-horn) *the shrilling horn* Heimdall's horn for sounding the alarm, which could be heard all over the world. 56, 144

Gna (gnaw) *bounteous* A lady-in-waiting to Frigg, she had a horse that could run through air and over water faster than the wind. 80

Gnomes Grumpy little men who lived in their own underground world and were marvelous miners and smiths. 36; characteristics, 24-25, 45-46; creation, 24; Freya's necklace, 84; gifts to the gods, 45-48 *see* Ivaldi, Sindri; golden boar, 61; Kvasir, 64-65; skill as smiths, 45-48

Goddesses 34-35, 80, 82; daughters, 73; first *see* Frigg; jewelry, 84 *See also* Asynjer

Gods *see* Aesir *and* Vanir

Gold 56; chessmen, 128, 150; Freya's tears, 63, 101; only for the living, 136; lust for, 140; sailors', 120; uses, 91

Golden boar 61

Grid (greed) *peace* A jotun woman who was the mother of Vidar, she loaned Thor weapons to protect himself with on his visit to the jotun Geirrod. 106, 107

Gullveig (*gule*-vay) *power of gold* A witch from Vanaheim who came to Asgard looking for gold, a visit that led to the war between the Aesir and the Vanir. 56, 58

Gungnir (*goong*-neer) *sounding* Odin's magic spear that never missed its mark. It was made by the sons of the gnome Ivaldi. 46, 73

Gunnlod (*gune*-lawd) *inviter to battle* The daughter of the jotun Suttung, she was the mother of Bragi. 64-66

Gymir (*gee*-meer) *noisy* A jotun, he was Gerd's father. 96-97

Healing goddess of, 80 *see* Eir

Heimdall (*hame*-dahl) *rainbow* The son of Odin and nine jotun maidens who were, perhaps, Aegir's nine daughters, he was the watchman of the Aesir, and stood guard at the top of the rainbow bridge to Asgard. 30, 56, 66, 86, 144; death, 147; Loki, 86; Thor's hammer, 101; trumpet-horn, 56 *see* Gjallarhorn

Hel (hel) *concealer* Offspring of Loki and Angerboda, she was the hag who ruled over the dead who had not fallen in battle. Her realm of the dead, also called Hel, was an underground replica of Odin's Valhalla, except for gruesome variations of decor. 10, 50, 128, 132, 142; Balder in, 132, 134; bridge to, 134-35; characteristics, 136

Hermod (*hehr*-mood) *courage in battle* A son of Odin, he was one of the war gods. 33, 134-36

Hod (hawd) *war* A son of Odin, and one of the war gods. He was blind, and personified force unguided by reason. Through Loki's treachery Hod inadvertently killed his half-brother Balder. 33, 77, 131, 138; characteristics, 77; in Hel, 136, return from, 150

Hodmimir (*hawd*-mee-meer) *bounteous man* The secret grove where Lif and Lifthrasir found refuge during the battle of Ragnarokk. 152

Hoenir (*heh*-neer) *hen-like* One of the three original Aesir gods who, with his brothers Odin and Lodur, created the world. Hoenir is called Vili (will) in the Poetic Edda. 21, 26, 150; birth, 18; characteristics, 58; home, 27; hostage to Vanir, 58-59; man, creation of, 26; marriage, 33

Honor 54, 71, 140

Hospitality 97; importance, 28; laws of, 117, 122

Hostages 58-60, 64

Hugi (*hue*-gee) *mind* A thought, in the form of the giant that Tjalfi raced at Utgardsloki's hall. 112, 116

Hymir (*hee*-meer) *the dark one* A jotun, he was lord of the wintry sea and Tyr's grandfather. Thor went to Hymir to get a cauldron for Aegir's feast. 120; daughter, 120, 125; Thor, 122, 124-26; wife, 120, 124

Hyrrokkin (*heer*-rawk-keen) *Shriveled by fire* The ogress who launched Balder's funeral ship. 132

Ice cow The second living creature, she provided food for Ymir and, by licking the brim of Ginungagap, uncovered the grandfather of Odin, Hoenir and Lodur. 14-16; bringing life, 17-18; death, 20

Iceland 11

Ida (*ee*-dah) *place of activity* The open green field in Asgard, around which stood the thirteen halls of the Aesir gods. It was here that the remaining Aesir gods gathered again after the destruction of Ragnarokk, nothing else of Asgard having survived. Field of, 36, 58, 68, 78, 150

Idunn (*ee*-doon) *rejuvenation* The wife of Bragi, she was the keeper of the apples of youth. She was kidnapped by the storm giant Tjasse. 66; apples of youth, 88-90

Ivaldi (*ee*-vahl-dee) *the mightiest one* The father of the gnomes who, at Loki's request, made Sif's new hair, Odin's spear, the Gungnir, and the ship, the Skidbladnir. 45, 46

Jotunheim (*yoh*-tun-hame) *home of the jotuns* The mountainous, glacial home of the giants—the jotuns and trolls. 10, 20, 27, 37, 38, 42, 96, 97, 100

Jotuns (*yoh*-tuns) *devourers* The giants that preceded the Aesir gods and had to be defeated before the world of the Aesir could be created. Personifications of the wild and destructive forces of nature and of winter in particular, they were usually enemies of both men and Aesir gods. They were thought of as having heads of stone and feet of ice, and some of them could change their shapes into those of eagles and wolves. They were also referred to as frost giants. 9-10; Aesir, relationship, 38; characteristics, 21, 42, 108; description, 14, 18; first (*see* Ymir); man, relationship, 38; mason, 68-71; storm (*see* Tjasse); Thor, 40. *See also* giants, frost giants

Knowledge, spirit of *see* Kvasir

Kvasir (*kva*-seer) *spittle* The spirit of intoxication and knowledge, his story was probably an agrarian myth in which his death provided life-giving nourishment as the cutting of grain provides bread. 64

Langobards (*lahn*-goh-bards) *long beards* A Germanic tribe that settled in Lombardy, in northern Italy. According to Norse mythology they received their name, long beards, because of a ruse suggested to them by Frigg. 82

Lidskjalf (*leed*-shahlf) *gate tower* Odin's throne on the tallest tower in Asgard, from which he could see the whole world. 37, 38, 50, 96, 138

Lif (leef) *life* The maiden who survived the destruction of Ragnarokk, along with the young man Lifthrasir. All the people of the new world were their descendants. 152

Lifthrasir (*leef*-thrah-seer) *stubborn will to survive* The young man who survived the destruction of Ragnarokk, along with the maiden Lif. *See* Lif. 152

Light-elves *See* Elves

Lin (leen) *head-dress* A lady-in-waiting to Frigg. 80

Lodur (*loh*-dure) *flame* One of the three original Aesir gods who, with his brothers Odin and Hoenir, created the world of the Aesir. In the Poetic Edda he is called Ve (sanctuary). 21, 26; birth, 18; home, 27; man, creation of, 26; marriage, 33

Logi (*loh*-gee) *flame* Wild fire, in the form of a giant with whom Loki had an eating contest at Utgardsloki's hall. 112, 116

Loki (*loh*-kee) *fire* Odin's jotun blood-brother, he had two wives, Sigunn in Asgard, and in Jotunheim, Angerboda, the mother of his three monstrous offspring, Hel, Fenris and the Midgard's Serpent. He was also the mother of Sleipnir. A personification of two aspects of fire, he suggested both the destructive conflagration and the helpful, warming flame. 42, 43, 138; Aesir, 45-46, wall, 68-69, 71; Balder, 130-31, 132; Brokk, 46-47, 49; characteristics, 42, 44, 128, 130, 137; children, 50; death, 147; disguises, 48, 136, 138, 139; fear, 138; Freya's necklace, 84, 86; Geirrod, 104-5; Heimdall, 86; Idunn's apples of youth, 88-89; Odin, 50, 137-38; punishment, 138-39, 140; revenge, 144; Sif's golden hair, 44-50; Skade, 91-92; Sleipnir, 71, 138; Thor, 45, 100-2, 107, 108; Utgardsloki, 112, 116; wives, 42, 139

Love goddess of, 62 *see* Freya

Magni (*mahg*-nee) *strength* Precociously strong son of Thor, he alone was able to rescue his father from the jotun Rungnir. He was one of the seven Aesir who survived Ragnarokk. 40, 119, 150

Man(kind) Aesir, relationship, 30; creation of, 25, 26-30; fate, 30

Mead An intoxicating drink made of water, honey and malt. 97, 98, 114, 117, 122, 126, 136

Midgard (*mid*-gahr) *middle dwelling place* The earth, which the first three Aesir gods made from Ymir's body and gave to human beings for their home. Yggdrasil, the world tree, grew from the middle of Midgard, and the rainbow bridge connected it to Asgard. 10; battles, 72-73; creation, 21; flowers, 31; mountains, 116

Midgard's Serpent (*mid*-gahr-*ser*-pent) A tremendous serpent, offspring of Loki and Angerboda, that lay at the bottom of the ocean, encircling the earth. 50, 116; at Ragnarokk, 144, 147; Thor, 122, 124

Mimir (*mee*-meer) *pondering* An ancient and wise jotun who shared his wisdom with Odin in return for one of Odin's eyes. He was beheaded by the Vanir, but Odin revived his head and Mimir continued to advise the Aesir. 38, 58-59

Mining 24-25

Mjolnir (*miohl*-neer) *the flashing crusher* Thor's magic hammer, known as the thunderbolt, that was made by the gnome Sindri. It crushed whatever it hit, and always flew back to Thor's hand. 40, 48-49

Modi (*moh*-dee) *courageous* A son of Thor, and one of the seven Aesir who survived Ragnarokk. 40, 150

Moon Given a masculine personality in the myths, the moon accordingly preceded the sun, a woman. 68; creation, 21; new, 151

Mountains origin, 118

Muspelheim (*moos*-pel-hame) *home of destruction* The home of the fire-demon Surt and his followers, it was shut outside the dome of the sky when the first three Aesir created their world. 10, 12, 21; ruler, 146

Nagelfar (*nahg*-el-fahr) *conveyance made of nails* The ship, made from dead men's nails, that brought ghosts to the battle of Ragnarokk. It was the ancient custom to cut short the nails of deceased persons and thereby prolong the time until Ragnarokk. 144

Nanna (*nah*-nah) *mother* or *the brave one* The wife of Balder and mother of Forsete, she was known for her constancy, even joining her husband in death. 54, 92; death, 132; in Hel, 136

New World The universe that came into existence after the destruction of the world of the Aesir on the day of Ragnarokk. 151-54

Nidhogg (*need*-hog) *hateful* The dragon of destruction that lay in deepest Niflheim gnawing at the root of the world tree, Yggdrasil. Nidhogg rose to the surface only after the world's destruction. 32, 50, 143, 150

Niflheim (*niff*-el-hame) *world of fog* The home of Nidhogg, the dragon of destruction, it was a place of frozen fog that the first three Aesir gods shoved deep underground where it wouldn't freeze Midgard. 12, 21, 32, 50, 134, 143

Night creation, 21

Njord (nioor) One of the Vanir fertility gods, he watched over wild fires and gave fair winds. He was the father of Frey and Freya, and his wife was Skade. His home was by the celestial sea, and no one knows where that was meant to have been. 59-60; marriage, 92-93

Norns (norns) *pronouncers* The three spirits of destiny who spun a thread of life for every human being and who cared for the world tree, Yggdrasil. Their names were Urd,

Verdande and Skuld, and their home was at the foot of Yggdrasil beside a magically pure well. 30, 143; ancestry, 30; home, 31; power, 30; world tree, 32-33
Noss (noss) *delight* Freya's daughter. 62
Od (odd) *ecstasy* Freya's vanished husband, often identified with Odin. 62
Odin (*oo*-den) *spirit, ecstasy* One of the three original Aesir gods who created the world, and subsequently the most important of all the gods. First among his wives was Frigg, and nine of the gods were his sons. Among other things he was god of war and god of wisdom, both intrepid and eloquent, and he was called by many names (*see* Ygg). The loss of an eye gave him inner sight, and his two ravens embodied his spirit soaring free of his body. In Germanic lands he was called Wothan, in England Woden. 10, 21, 26; All-father, 33; arm ring *see* Draupnir; Balder, 132; birth, 18; bloodbrother, 137-38 *see* Loki; characteristics, 38, 90, 117; duties, 128; family, 33; fatherhood, 33; favorite island, 82 *see* Fyn; guesthouse, 73 *see* Valhalla; god of storm and war, 72, 73 *see* Ygg; heroes, 73, 77, 80, 150 *see* Valhalla; home, 27; honor, 71, 140; Loki, 42, 50, 52; man, creation of, 26, 28; marriage, 33; Mimir, 38; poetry, 65-66; position, 140; power, 33, 38, 44; at Ragnarokk, 144, 146-47; sons, 52, 54, 56, 77, 150; spear, 46, 73 *see* Gungnir; steed, 71, 72, 117 *see* Sleipnir; throne, 37, 38, 50, 96, 138 *see* Lidskjalf; volva, 128; wisdom, 33, 38; warrior maidens, 73 *see* Valkyries; wives, 37, 80; Yggdrasil, 33-34
Old age personification, 116 *see* Elle
Peace settlement of pact, 64
Poetry creation, 64-66; god of, 66 *see* Bragi
Population earthly-godly 33
Ragnarokk (*rahg*-nah-rock) *destiny of the gods* The destiny, which was destruction, of the Aesir gods. A mistranslation of this word led to the familiar, but erroneous, term "the twilight of the gods." There is a possibility that Ragnarokk was tacked onto Norse mythology as part of Christianity's attack on paganism in Scandinavia. Certainly it is an unusual feature for a mythology to include the total destruction of its gods, and the new world with its one god sounds like an after-the-fact description of Christianity's triumph over the pagan beliefs. The possibility is strengthened by the fact that the myths were written down when Christianity was established in northern Europe and Iceland. *See* Edda, Gimlé 10, 140, 142-44, 146-47, 150, 152
Rain 21; giver of *see* Frey
Rainbow bridge The bridge between Asgard and the earth, which icy jotuns and trolls could not climb because the red in it was fire. 35, 36, 56, 146
Rân (rahn) *plunder* An ogress who ransacked sunken ships, she was the wife of the jotun Aegir. 120
Ratatosk (*rah*-tah-tosk) *gnawing tooth* A squirrel who scampered about in Yggdrasil, the world tree, spreading gossip. 32
Rune (*roo*-neh) *that which is secret* Any of the ancient symbols used both for magic and for writing. They were perhaps derived from an old Germanic alphabet, which was in turn perhaps suggested by a Greek script. A number of stone tablets with memorial inscriptions written in the Runic alphabet have been found by archeologists working in northern Europe. 98
Rungnir (*roonq*-neer) *noise-maker* A jotun who challenged Thor to a duel. He was perhaps a stone age thunder demon who was displaced by Thor. 117, 118-19
Runic alphabet 33
Sacrifices 33, 34
Saga (*sah*-gah) *story* A goddess identified with Frigg. 82
Sea lord of *see* Aegir
Sif (seef) *kinship* The wife of Thor, she was the goddess of household and family ties. Her long golden hair represented the golden fields of grain. 40, 117, 138; golden hair, 44-45
Sigunn (*see*-goon) *victory-giver* Loki's wife in Asgard. 42, 139
Sindri (*sin*-dree) *cinder* A gnome, the brother of Brokk, who fashioned Odin's armring, the Draupnir, Frey's golden boar, and Thor's hammer, the Mjolnir. 47-48
Sjaelland (*shell*-lahn) A Danish island said to have been created by Gefjon. It is the site of Copenhagen, capital of Denmark. 83 *see* Copenhagen
Skade (*skah*-deh) *damage* The daughter of the jotun Tjasse, who went to Asgard to avenge her father's death and ended up the wife of Njord. She was the goddess of skiers. 91-95; husband, 91-93
Skidbladnir (*shee*-blahd-neer) *made of wood slats* Frey's magic ship that was made by the sons of the gnome Ivaldi. It could change size, and sailed over land and sea, and represented a bright summer cloud. 46
Skiers god of, 94-95 *see* Ull
Ski-goddess *see* Skade
Skirnir (*sheer*-neer) *he who makes things shine* Frey's faithful servant who wooed Gerd for his master. In return Frey gave Skirnir his sword and so had no weapon to defend himself at the battle of Ragnarokk. 97-98
Skrymir (*skree*-meer) *frightener* The jotun Utgardsloki disguised as a giant to outwit Thor. 110-11, 112, 116
Skuld (skule) *future, duty* One of the three Norns. 30, 31, 32
Sleipnir (*slep*-neer) *the glider* Odin's eight-legged horse, offspring of Loki. 71, 72, 117, 134, 135, 136, 138
Spirit 18 *see* Odin
Spirits creation 25
Sprites creation 25
Stars creation 21
Starvation 142
Storm jotun *see* Tjasse
Sturluson, Snorri Author of the Prose Edda. 11
Sun The sun was considered feminine because she provided life-giving warmth. 68; creation, 21; new, 151
Sunshine giver of *see* Frey
Surt (soort) *black* A fire-demon, the ruler of Muspelheim, who burst through a crack in the dome of the sky to participate in the battle of Ragnarokk. 146, 147, 150
Suttung (*soot*-tung) *heavy with broth* A jotun, father of Gunnlod. 64, 66
Sweden 82
Thokk (thock) *thanks* Loki disguised as the old crone who refused to weep Balder out of Hel. 136
Thor (*thore* or *ture*) *thunder* The thunder god and strongest of the Aesir, he was a son of Odin and a jotun maiden who personified the earth. Thus Thor represented the union of heaven and earth. His hammer, Mjolnir the thunderbolt, not only kept the jotuns at bay, it also blessed weddings, and Thor's day, Thursday, was preferred for a wedding day. The stories about Thor often stand between true myth and fairy tales. 10, 33, 40, 70, 137; Aegir, 120, 126; Balder, 132; characteristics, 40, 122, 124-25, 138; drinking horn, 117; duties, 128, 142; Geirrod, 105, 107; glutton, 105, 107, 122; hammer, 40, 48-49, 108, 110, theft of, 100-2; Hymir, 122, 124-26; Loki, 45, 108, 138, 139; Midgard's Serpent, 122, 124; power, 44; at Ragnarokk, 144, 147; Rungnir, 118-19; servant, 108 *see* Tjalfi; shame, 115, 116; Skrymir, 110-11, 112, 116; sons, 40, 119, 150; Utgardsloki, 108, 111-16
Thought personification, 116 *see* Hugi
Thrym (thrim) *noisy* A jotun who stole Thor's hammer, and refused to return it until Freya came to Jotunheim to be his bride. 100, 102

Thunder 102; god of, 40 *see* Thor
Tjalfi (ti*ahl*-fee) *the toiler* The swiftest of runners, he was Thor's servant. 108, 110, 118, 119; Utgardsloki, 112, 116
Tjasse (ti*ahs*-ser) The storm giant who kidnapped Idunn and her apples of youth. He was the father of Skade. 87-89; daughter, 91; death, 90
Trees in Asgard, 73; creation of man, 26-27; world *see* Yggdrasil
Troll knot 116
Trolls Members of the jotun race, some of whom had many, many heads. 97, 125; characteristics, 16, 18, 21; Thor, 40, 70
Tyr (teer) *shining* The son of Odin and a jotun maiden, and grandson of the jotun Hymir, he was god of the sword and of duelling. He had to lose his right hand when he broke his sacred word to Fenris the wolf, because that was the customary punishment in those days. 10, 30, 52, 77, 120, 124; characteristics, 77; death, 147; loss of hand, 52; mother, 122, 125
Ull (ool) *the shaggy one* The god of skiers, and a very ancient god, he was incorporated into the cult of the Aesir as the son of Sif. Judging from the number of places in Scandinavia that contain his name, he was once an important deity, but he was virtually forgotten by the time the myths were written down, and there are no stories about him. (*see* Edda) 94-95
Urd (oord) *fate* One of the three Norns. 30, 31, 32
Utgard (*oot*-gahr) *outer place* Home of Utgardsloki. 115
Utgardsloki (*oot*-gahrs-loh-kee) *Loki of the outer world* The strongest and slyest of the jotuns, he outwitted Thor. 108, 111-16
Valhalla (*vahl*-hahl-lah) *hall of slain warriors* The vast hall in Asgard where Odin's army of fallen heroes lived. 73, 76-79, 80, 117, 140; at Ragnarokk, 144
Vali (*vah*-lee) *terrible* The youngest of Odin's sons, he was one of the gods of war. He was one of the seven Aesir to survive Ragnarokk. 33, 77, 136, 150
Valkyries (vahl-*kure*-rees) *choosers of the fallen heroes* Odin's warrior maidens who chose which warriors should die in battle, carried the slain men to Valhalla, and looked after them there. There were six, nine, or thirteen of them at a time, and they had warlike names such as "the storm raiser" and "witch of the shield." 73, 76, 91, 140; duties, 128
Vanaheim (*vah*-nah-hame) *home of the Vanir* The home of the Vanir gods. 10, 21
Vanir (*vah*-neer) *friendly* These were probably Bronze Age gods of fertility whose cult originated in a milder climate. They were, it is thought, superceded in the Iron Age by the cult of the Aesir, gods of storm and war. The battle of the Aesir and the Vanir that led to the arrival in Asgard of Njord, Frey and Freya reflects the ancient merging of these two cults. 56, 150; Aesir relationship, 58-59, 64; characteristics, 58; reign, 21
Var (vahr) *truth or promise* The goddess of faithfulness between man and woman. 80
Verdande (*vahr*-ah-nay) *that which is to come* One of the three Norns. 30, 31, 32
Vidar (*vee*-dahr) *ruler of large territories* The son of Odin and the jotun woman Grid, he was one of the gods of war. At the battle of Ragnarokk he had the honor of avenging his father's death. His weapon was an enormous boot made, it was said, of the scraps of leather that good men trimmed from the toes and heels when they were making their own shoes. 33, 77, 106, 147, 150
Vigrid (*vee*-gree) *the field where one rides to battle* The largest field in the world, where the battle of Ragnarokk took place. No one knows where it was meant to have been. 146
Volva (*vohl*-vah) *carrier of a magic staff* A prophetess or sybil. In the Poetic Edda, a volva tells Odin the outline of Aesir history, from primeval chaos to the grim description of Ragnarokk, asking him periodically "do you know more now, or not?" 128, 140
Warrior maidens 73 *see* Valkyries
Wars 82, 140 *see also* Battles
Well of Wisdom A well in Jotunheim owned by the jotun Mimir that contained the knowledge of the jotun race. 38, 42
Wild-fire personification, 116 *see* Logi
Wisdom god of, 33, 38 *see* Odin
Witches 33, 56, 97; burning, 56 *see* Gullveig
World creation, 21-25 *see also* Midgard
Ygg (eeg) *terrible one* The name of Odin as the god of storm and war. 72, 73
Yggdrasil (*eeg*-drah-sil) *Odin's steed* The world tree, an enormous ash that grew in the middle of the world and was sacred to Odin. Mythically the embodiment of the universe, its survival was necessary for the survival of the Aesir world. The Christmas tree descends from the world tree, and many of its traditional decorations were adapted from Norse mythology: candles for Thor's flashing lightning, and garlands for the rainbow bridge to Asgard. At the top, instead of the pagan eagle, the Christmas angel keeps watch; and at the bottom, the Christ child in his crib replaces the Norns as the Christian's arbiter of human destiny. 10, 31-35, 140; council at, 89, 128; dragon, 50; fall, 150; Odin, 33-34, 42; at Ragnarokk, 143
Ymir (*ee*-meer) *resounding* The first living being and the progenitor of the jotuns, he emerged from Ginungagap accompanied by his ice-cow. He was slain by the first three Aesir gods and Midgard was made of his body. 14-17, 21; birth, 14; characteristics, 18; death, 20; offspring, 16, 20
Youth Idunn's apples of 88-89

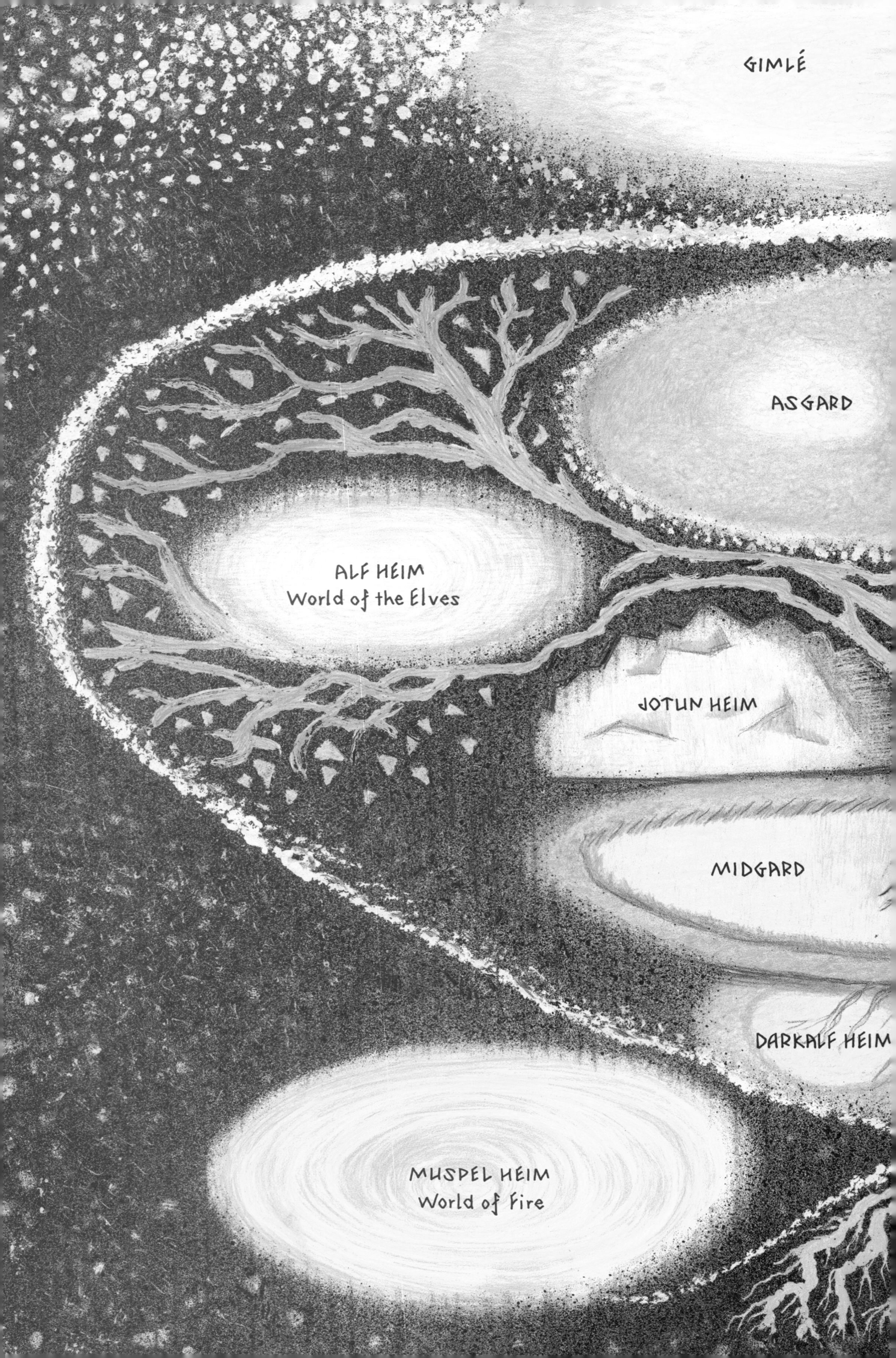

GIMLÉ

ASGARD

ALF HEIM
World of the Elves

JOTUN HEIM

MIDGARD

DARKALF HEIM

MUSPEL HEIM
World of Fire

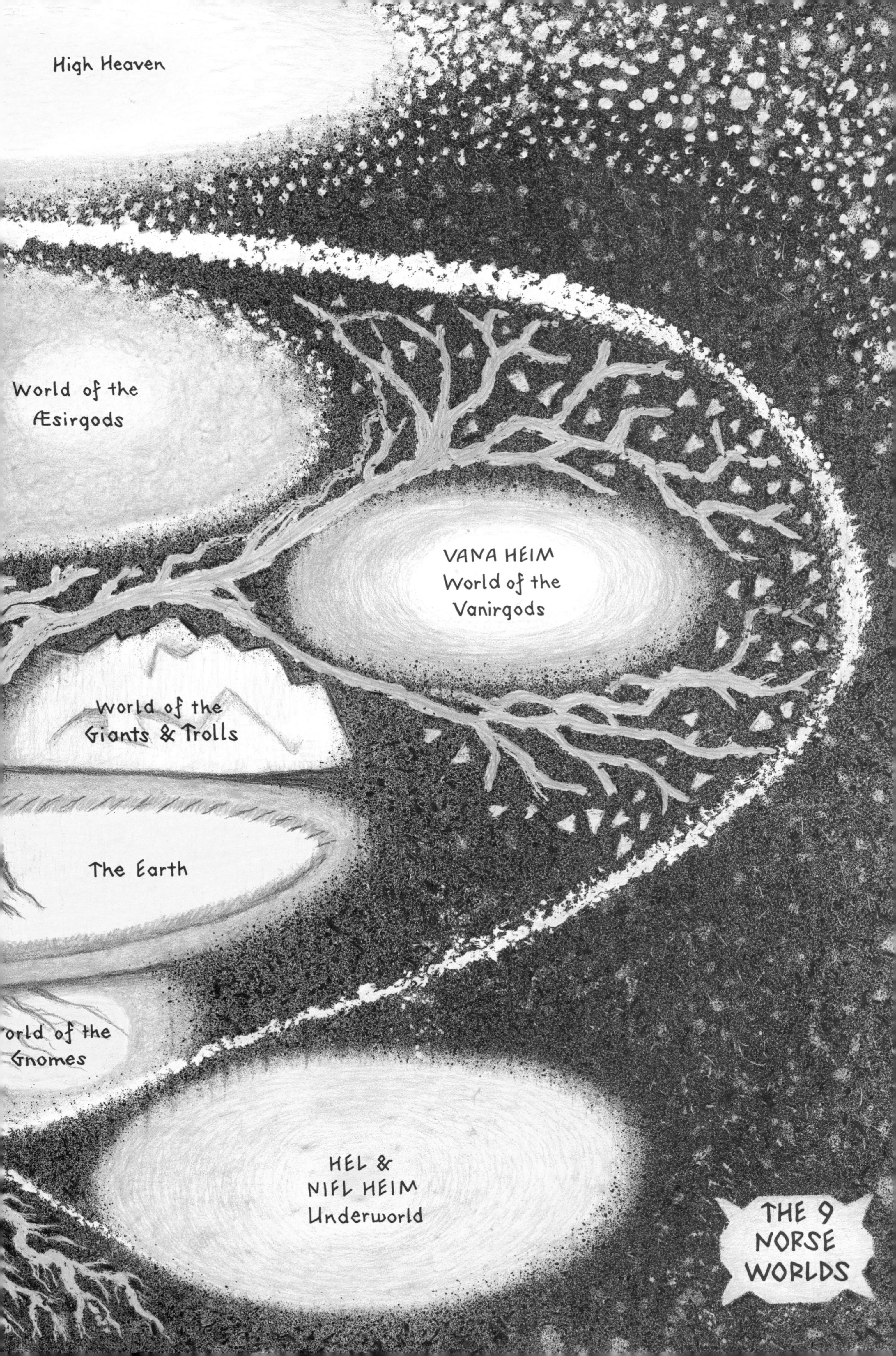

THE 9 NORSE WORLDS

High Heaven

World of the
Æsirgods

VANA HEIM
World of the
Vanirgods

World of the
Giants & Trolls

The Earth

orld of the
Gnomes

HEL &
NIFL HEIM
Underworld